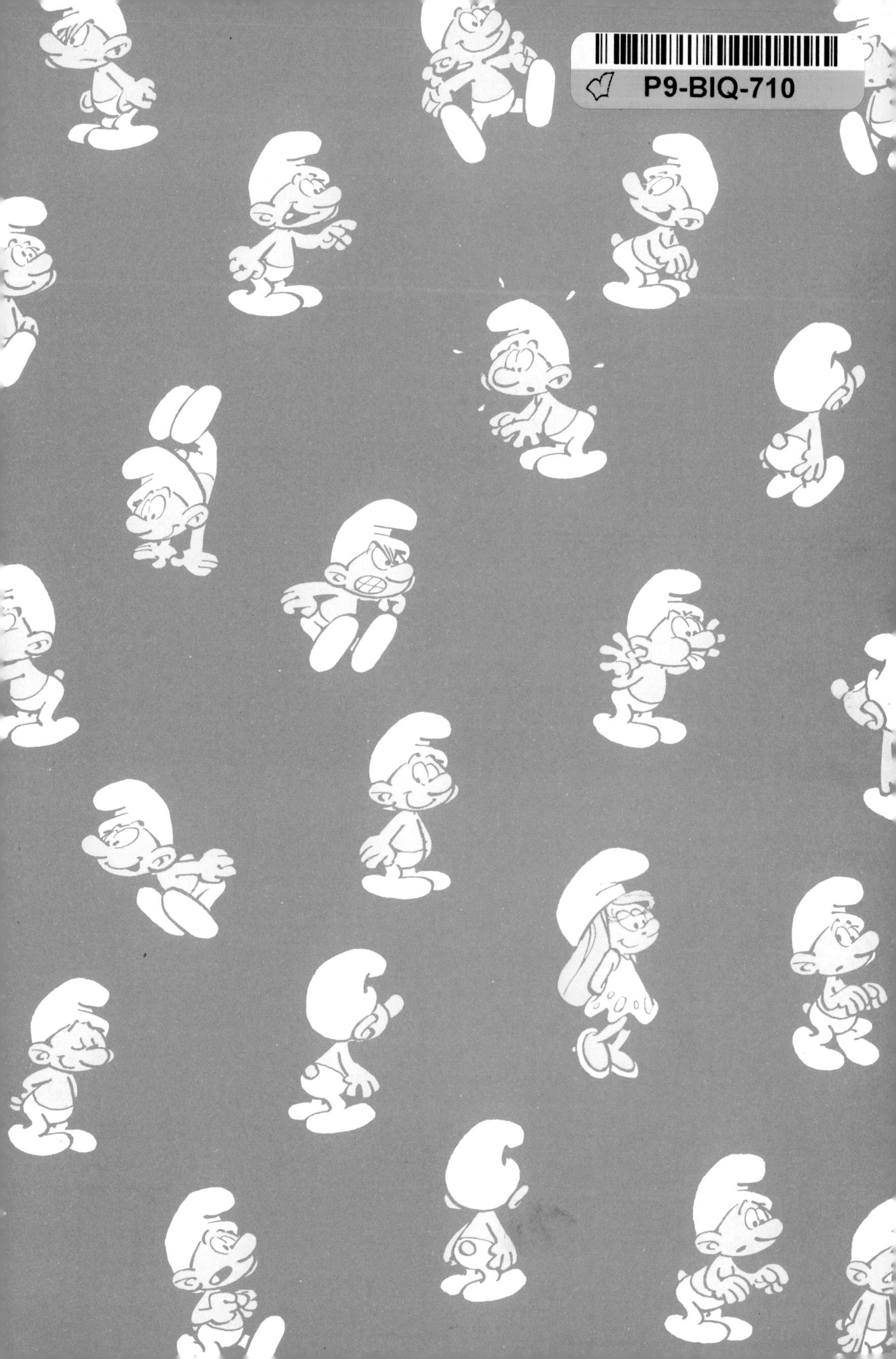

THE SMURFETTE

Peyo

THE SMURFETTE

Tralalee la la
WIIIEEEEEEE
What's wrong?
What's smurfing on?
There! A horrible beast!!
Where is it? Where is it?
THERE!
?
HAVE NO FEAR, SMURFETTE. I'LL MAKE THIS MONSTER GO AWAY!
Go on! Pshhh! Scram!!
You're so brave! You saved my life!
It's dangerous to smurf alone in the forest!
We'll keep you company!
To protect you!

A SMURFS GRAPHIC NOVEL BY Peyo

PAPERCUTZ™
NEW YORK

SMURFS GRAPHIC NOVELS AVAILABLE FROM PAPERCUTZ™

PURPLE SMURFS
THE SMURFS AND THE MAGIC FLUTE
THE SMURF KING
THE SMURFETTE
THE SMURFS AND THE EGG
THE SMURFS AND THE HOWLIBIRD

1. **THE PURPLE SMURFS**
2. **THE SMURFS AND THE MAGIC FLUTE**
3. **THE SMURF KING**
4. **THE SMURFETTE**
5. **THE SMURFS AND THE EGG**
6. **THE SMURFS AND THE HOWLIBIRD**

COMING SOON:

THE ASTRO SMURF
THE SMURF APPRENTICE
GARGAMEL AND THE SMURFS

7. **THE ASTROSMURF**
8. **THE SMURF APPRENTICE**
9. **GARGAMEL AND THE SMURFS**

The Smurfs graphic novels are available in paperback for $5.99 each and in hardcover for $10.99 each. Please add $4.00 for postage and handling for the first book, add $1.00 for each additional book.

Please make check payable to:
NBM Publishing

Send to:
PAPERCUTZ, 40 Exchange Place, Suite 1308
New York, NY 10005 [1-800-886-1223]

WWW.PAPERCUTZ.COM

THE SMURFETTE

"The Smurfette"
BY YVAN DELPORTE AND PEYO

"The Hungry Smurfs"
BY YVAN DELPORTE AND PEYO

Joe Johnson, *SMURFLATIONS*
Adam Grano, *SMURFIC DESIGN*
Janice Chiang, *LETTERING SMURFETTE*
Matt. Murray, *SMURF CONSULTANT*
Michael Petranek, *ASSOCIATE SMURF*
Jim Salicrup, *SMURF-IN-CHIEF*

PAPERBACK EDITION ISBN: 978-1-59707-236-6
HARDCOVER EDITION ISBN: 978-1-59707-237-3

PRINTED IN CHINA APRIL 2011 BY WKT CO. LTD
3/F PHASE I LEADER INDUSTRIAL CENTRE
188 TEXACO ROAD, TSEUN WAN, N.T., HONG KONG

DISTRIBUTED BY MACMILLAN
SECOND PAPERCUTZ PRINTING

THE SMURFETTE

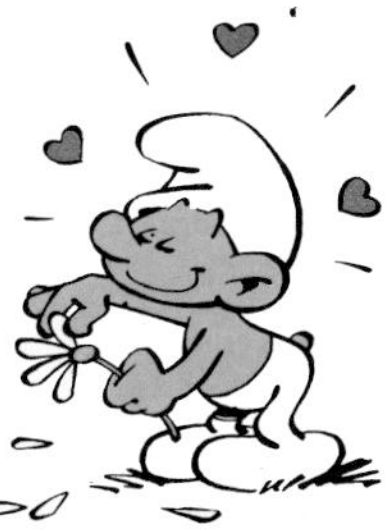

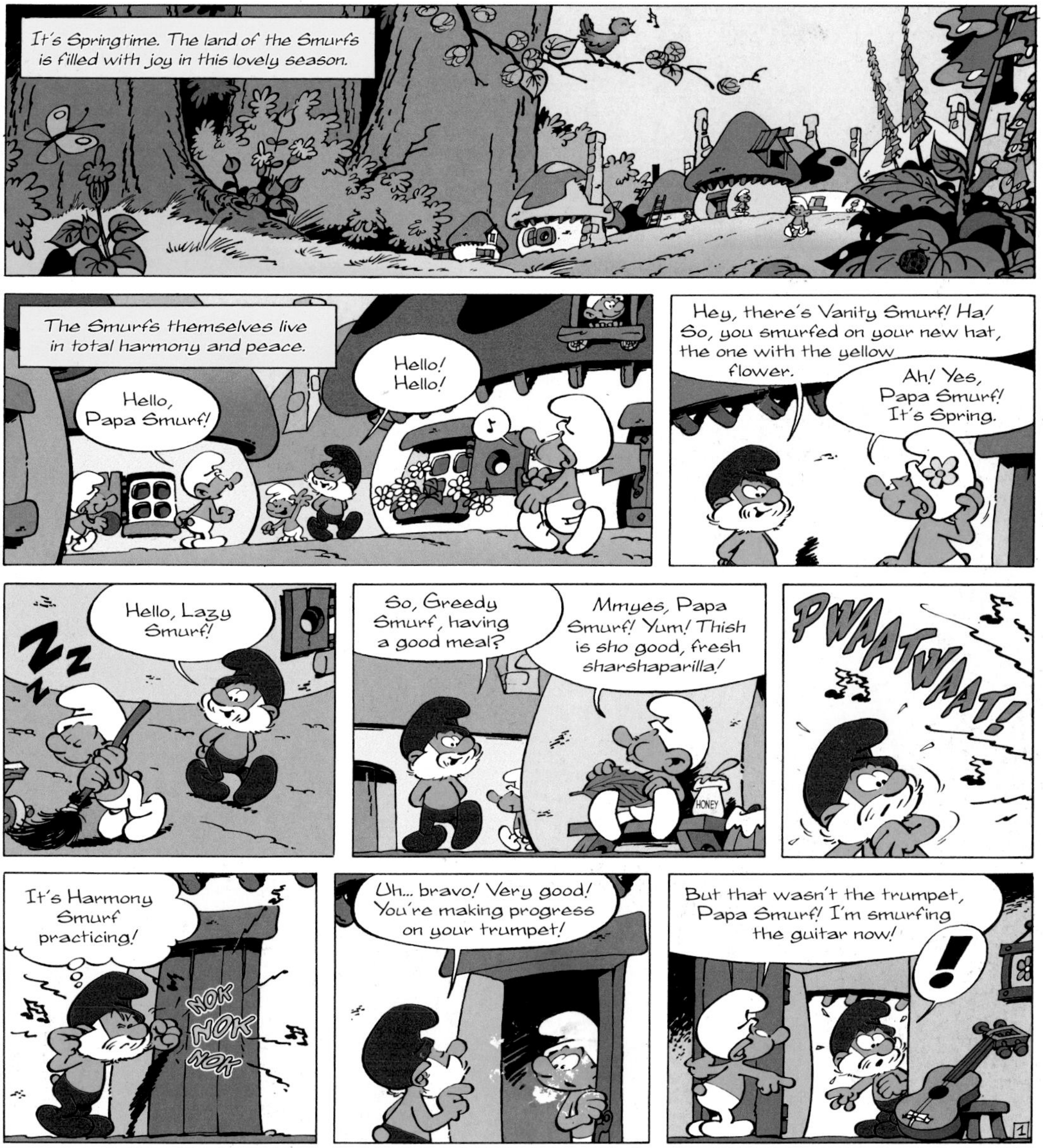

It's Springtime. The land of the Smurfs is filled with joy in this lovely season.
The Smurfs themselves live in total harmony and peace.
Hello, Papa Smurf!
Hello! Hello!
Hey, there's Vanity Smurf! Ha! So, you smurfed on your new hat, the one with the yellow flower.
Ah! Yes, Papa Smurf! It's Spring.
Hello, Lazy Smurf!
So, Greedy Smurf, having a good meal?
Mmyes, Papa Smurf! Yum! Thish is sho good, fresh sharshaparilla!
HONEY
PWAATWAAT!
It's Harmony Smurf practicing!
NOK NOK NOK
Uh... bravo! Very good! You're making progress on your trumpet!
But that wasn't the trumpet, Papa Smurf! I'm smurfing the guitar now!
!
1

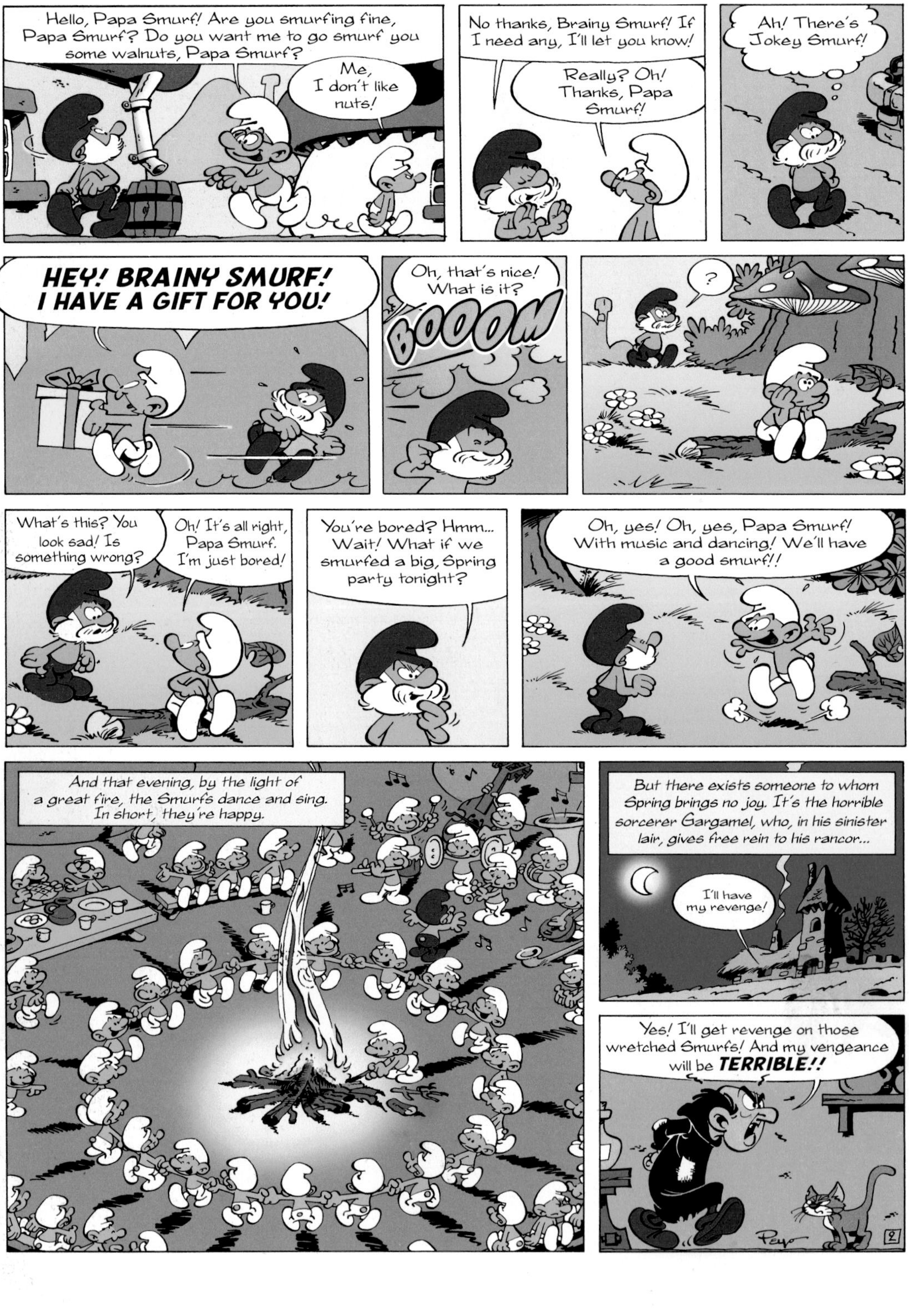
Hello, Papa Smurf! Are you smurfing fine, Papa Smurf? Do you want me to go smurf you some walnuts, Papa Smurf?
Me, I don't like nuts!
No thanks, Brainy Smurf! If I need any, I'll let you know!
Really? Oh! Thanks, Papa Smurf!
Ah! There's Jokey Smurf!
HEY! BRAINY SMURF! I HAVE A GIFT FOR YOU!
Oh, that's nice! What is it?
BOOOM
?
What's this? You look sad! Is something wrong?
Oh! It's all right, Papa Smurf. I'm just bored!
You're bored? Hmm... Wait! What if we smurfed a big, Spring party tonight?
Oh, yes! Oh, yes, Papa Smurf! With music and dancing! We'll have a good smurf!!
And that evening, by the light of a great fire, the Smurfs dance and sing. In short, they're happy.
But there exists someone to whom Spring brings no joy. It's the horrible sorcerer Gargamel, who, in his sinister lair, gives free rein to his rancor...
I'll have my revenge!
Yes! I'll get revenge on those wretched Smurfs! And my vengeance will be TERRIBLE!!
Peyo
2

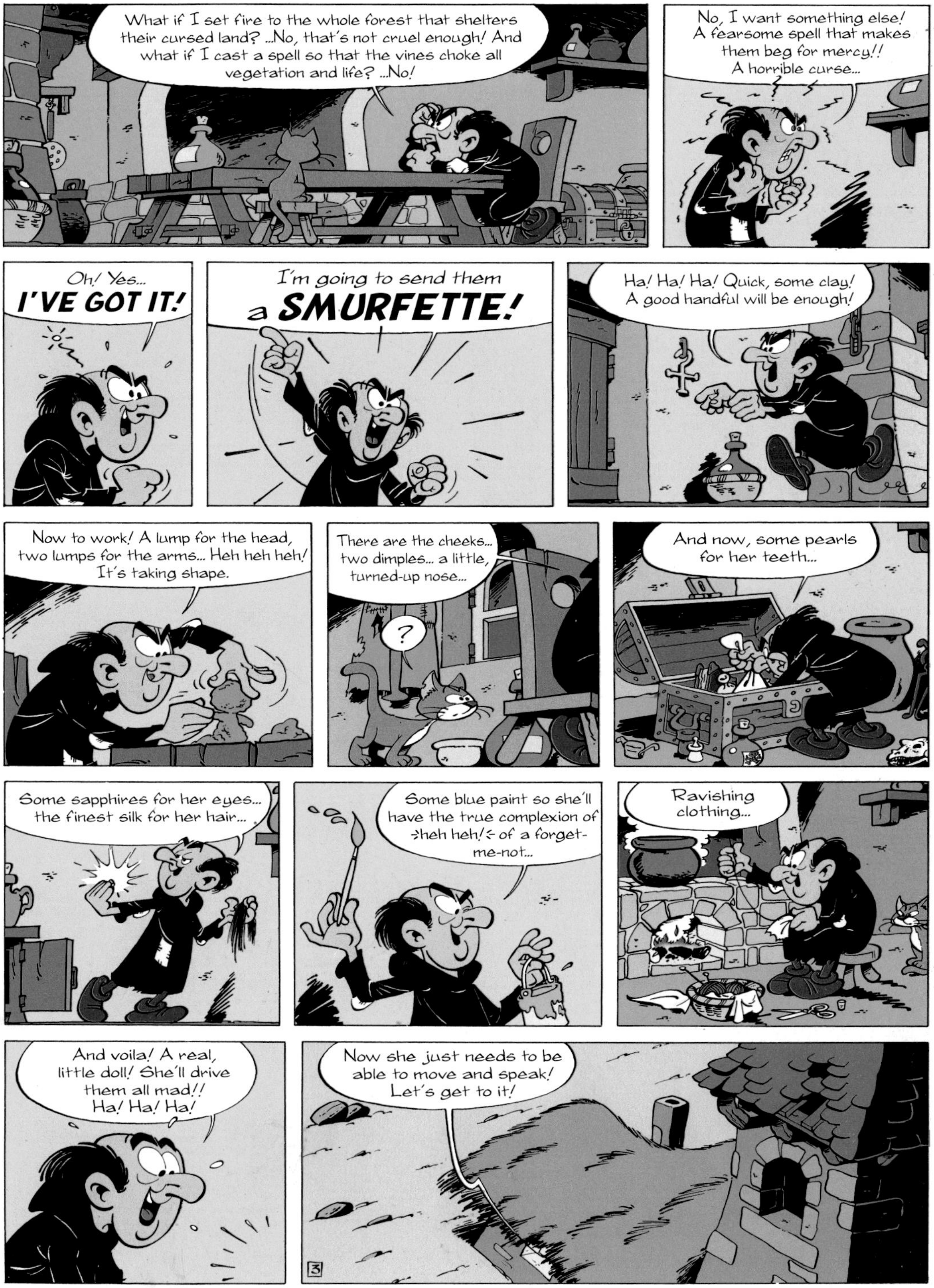
What if I set fire to the whole forest that shelters their cursed land? ...No, that's not cruel enough! And what if I cast a spell so that the vines choke all vegetation and life? ...No!
No, I want something else! A fearsome spell that makes them beg for mercy!! A horrible curse...
Oh! Yes... I'VE GOT IT!
I'm going to send them a SMURFETTE!
Ha! Ha! Ha! Quick, some clay! A good handful will be enough!
Now to work! A lump for the head, two lumps for the arms... Heh heh heh! It's taking shape.
There are the cheeks... two dimples... a little, turned-up nose...
?
And now, some pearls for her teeth...
Some sapphires for her eyes... the finest silk for her hair...
Some blue paint so she'll have the true complexion of →heh heh!← of a forget-me-not...
Ravishing clothing...
And voila! A real, little doll! She'll drive them all mad!! Ha! Ha! Ha!
Now she just needs to be able to move and speak! Let's get to it!
3

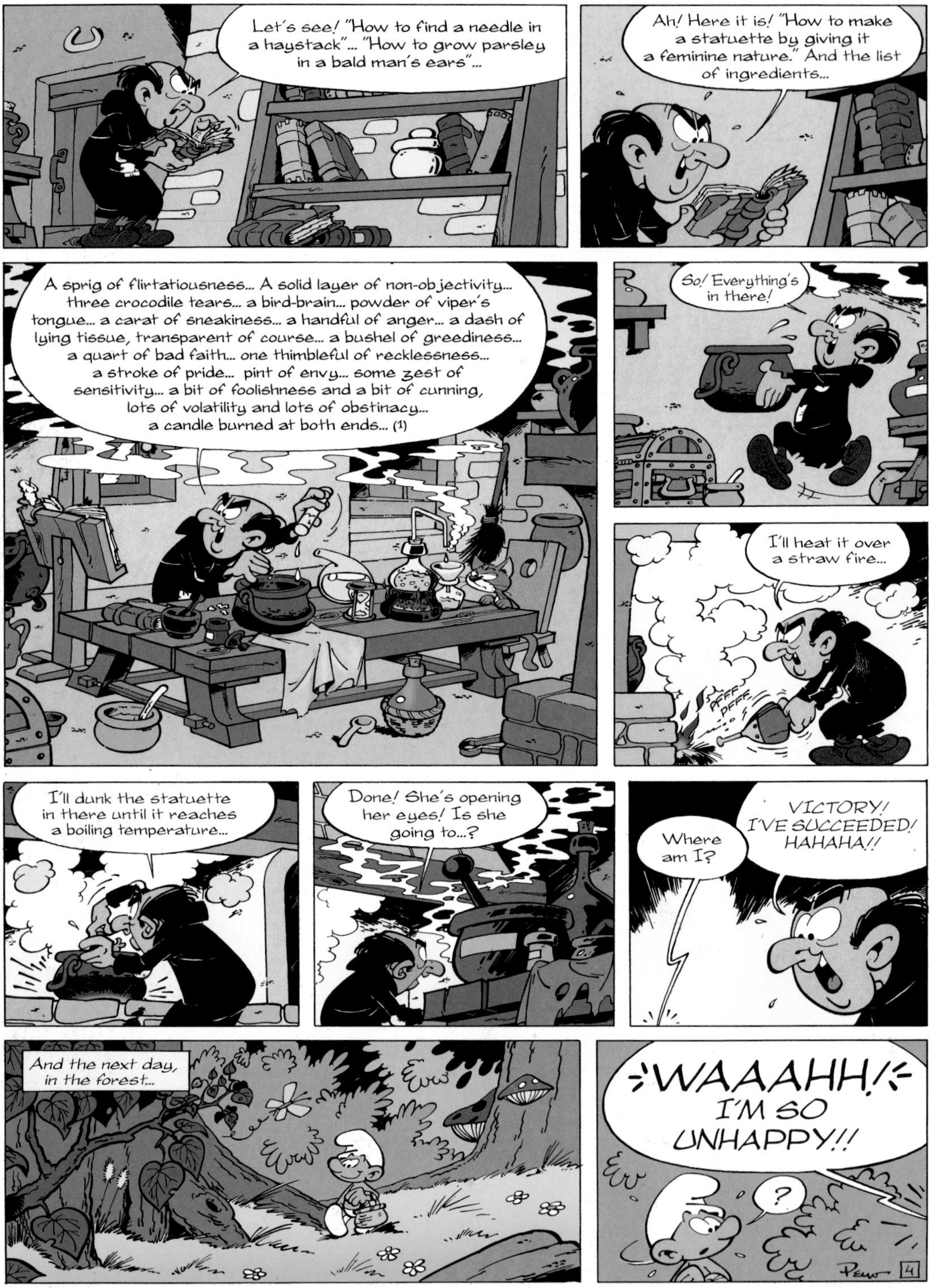

Let's see! "How to find a needle in a haystack"... "How to grow parsley in a bald man's ears"...
Ah! Here it is! "How to make a statuette by giving it a feminine nature." And the list of ingredients...
A sprig of flirtatiousness... A solid layer of non-objectivity... three crocodile tears... a bird-brain... powder of viper's tongue... a carat of sneakiness... a handful of anger... a dash of lying tissue, transparent of course... a bushel of greediness... a quart of bad faith... one thimbleful of recklessness... a stroke of pride... pint of envy... some zest of sensitivity... a bit of foolishness and a bit of cunning, lots of volatility and lots of obstinacy... a candle burned at both ends... (1)
So! Everything's in there!
I'll heat it over a straw fire...
PFFF PFFF
I'll dunk the statuette in there until it reaches a boiling temperature...
Done! She's opening her eyes! Is she going to...?
Where am I?
VICTORY! I'VE SUCCEEDED! HAHAHA!!
And the next day, in the forest...
WAAAHH! I'M SO UNHAPPY!!
?
4

(1) This text is the sole responsibility of the author of the spell-book "Magicae Formulae," Beelzebub Editions.

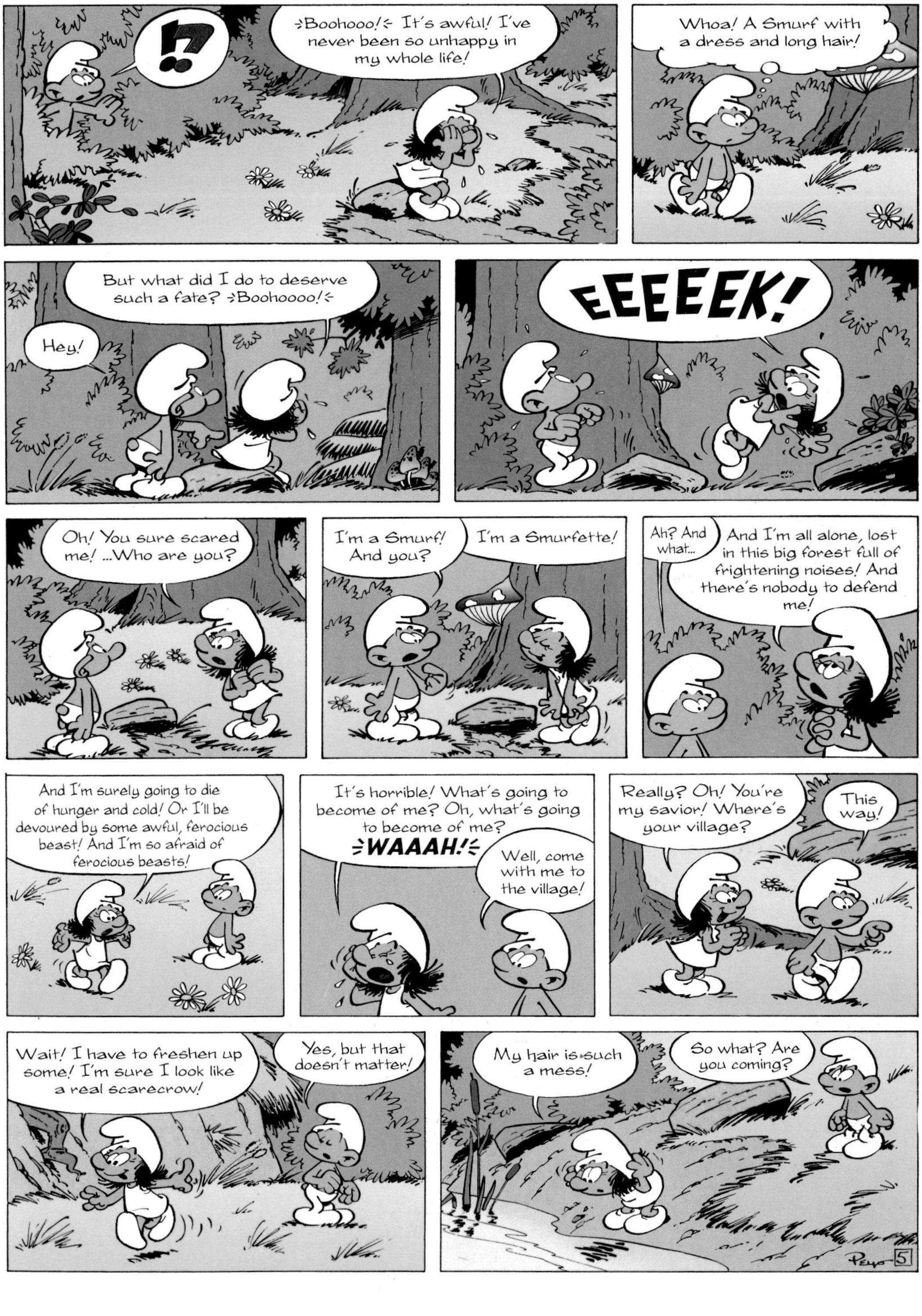
!?
≥Boohooo!≤ It's awful! I've never been so unhappy in my whole life!
Whoa! A Smurf with a dress and long hair!
But what did I do to deserve such a fate? ≥Boohoooo!≤
Hey!
EEEEEK!
Oh! You sure scared me! ...Who are you?
I'm a Smurf! And you?
I'm a Smurfette!
Ah? And what...
And I'm all alone, lost in this big forest full of frightening noises! And there's nobody to defend me!
And I'm surely going to die of hunger and cold! Or I'll be devoured by some awful, ferocious beast! And I'm so afraid of ferocious beasts!
It's horrible! What's going to become of me? Oh, what's going to become of me? ≥WAAAH!≤
Well, come with me to the village!
Really? Oh! You're my savior! Where's your village?
This way!
Wait! I have to freshen up some! I'm sure I look like a real scarecrow!
Yes, but that doesn't matter!
My hair is such a mess!
So what? Are you coming?

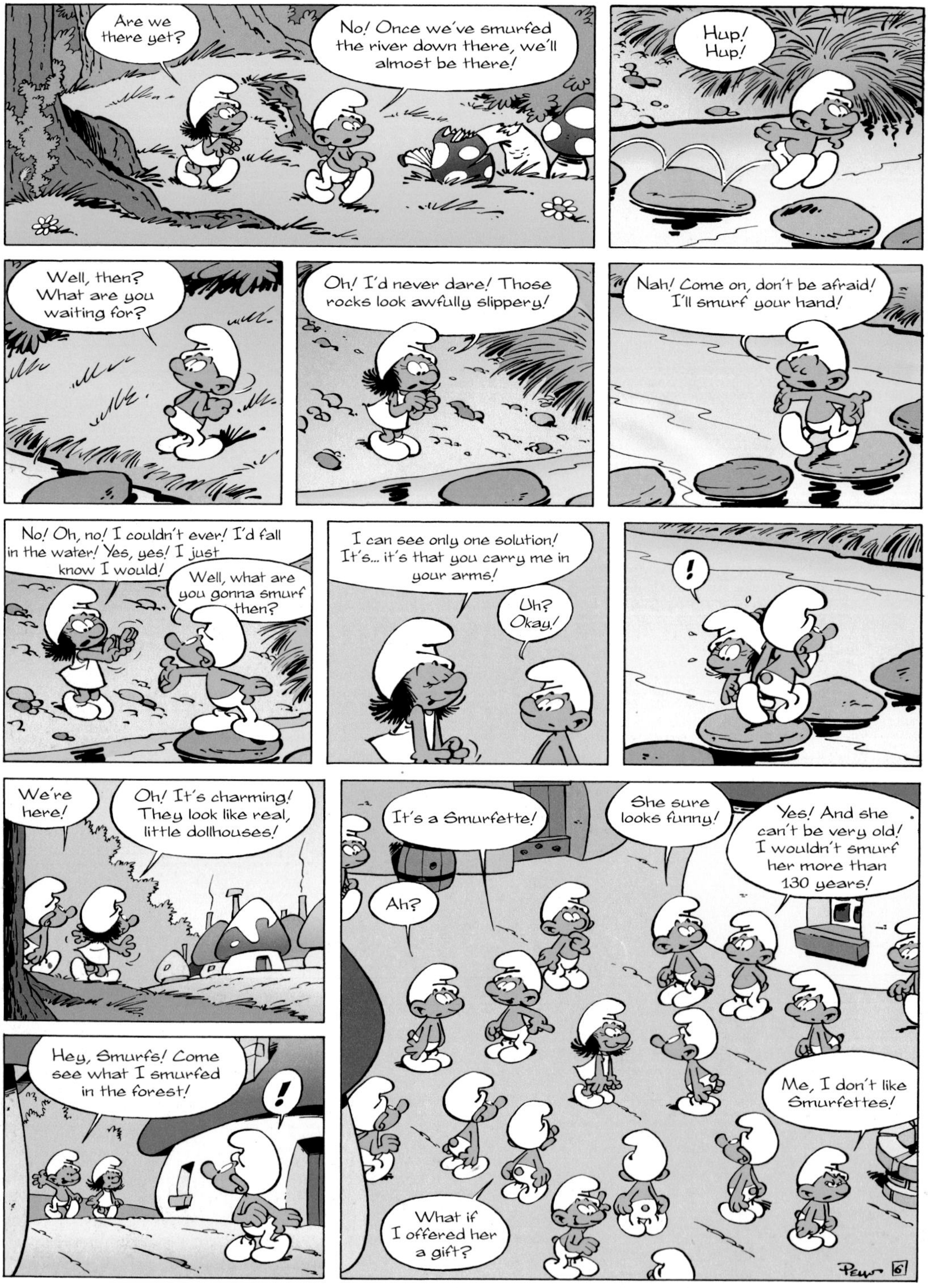

Are we there yet?
No! Once we've smurfed the river down there, we'll almost be there!
Hup! Hup!
Well, then? What are you waiting for?
Oh! I'd never dare! Those rocks look awfully slippery!
Nah! Come on, don't be afraid! I'll smurf your hand!
No! Oh, no! I couldn't ever! I'd fall in the water! Yes, yes! I just know I would!
Well, what are you gonna smurf then?
I can see only one solution! It's... it's that you carry me in your arms!
Uh? Okay!
!
We're here!
Oh! It's charming! They look like real, little dollhouses!
Hey, Smurfs! Come see what I smurfed in the forest!
!
It's a Smurfette!
Ah?
She sure looks funny!
Yes! And she can't be very old! I wouldn't smurf her more than 130 years!
Me, I don't like Smurfettes!
What if I offered her a gift?

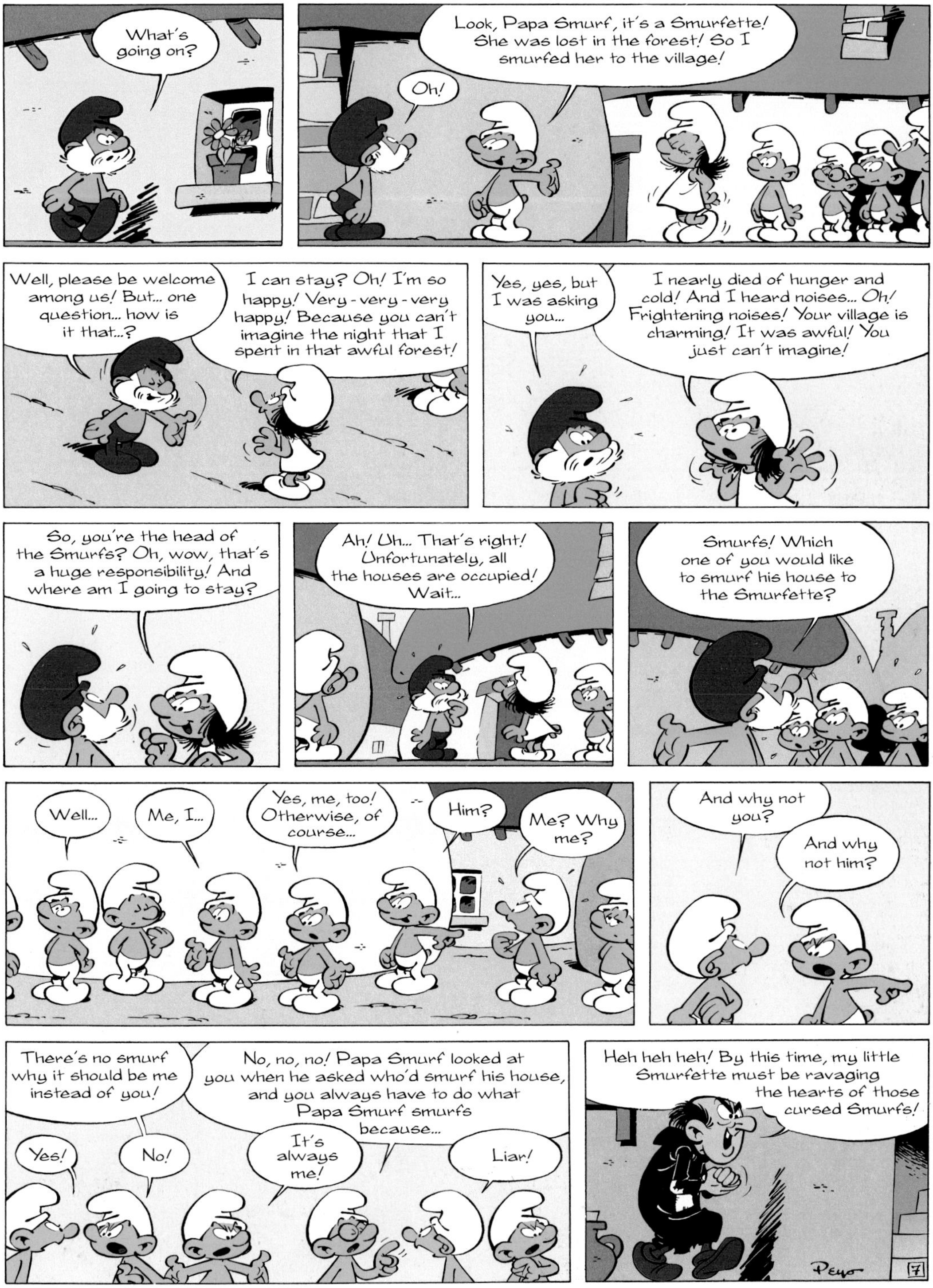
What's going on?
Look, Papa Smurf, it's a Smurfette! She was lost in the forest! So I smurfed her to the village!
Oh!
Well, please be welcome among us! But... one question... how is it that...?
I can stay? Oh! I'm so happy! Very-very-very happy! Because you can't imagine the night that I spent in that awful forest!
Yes, yes, but I was asking you...
I nearly died of hunger and cold! And I heard noises... Oh! Frightening noises! Your village is charming! It was awful! You just can't imagine!
So, you're the head of the Smurfs? Oh, wow, that's a huge responsibility! And where am I going to stay?
Ah! Uh... That's right! Unfortunately, all the houses are occupied! Wait...
Smurfs! Which one of you would like to smurf his house to the Smurfette?
Well...
Me, I...
Yes, me, too! Otherwise, of course...
Him?
Me? Why me?
And why not you?
And why not him?
There's no smurf why it should be me instead of you!
No, no, no! Papa Smurf looked at you when he asked who'd smurf his house, and you always have to do what Papa Smurf smurfs because...
Yes!
No!
It's always me!
Liar!
Heh heh heh! By this time, my little Smurfette must be ravaging the hearts of those cursed Smurfs!
Peyo
7

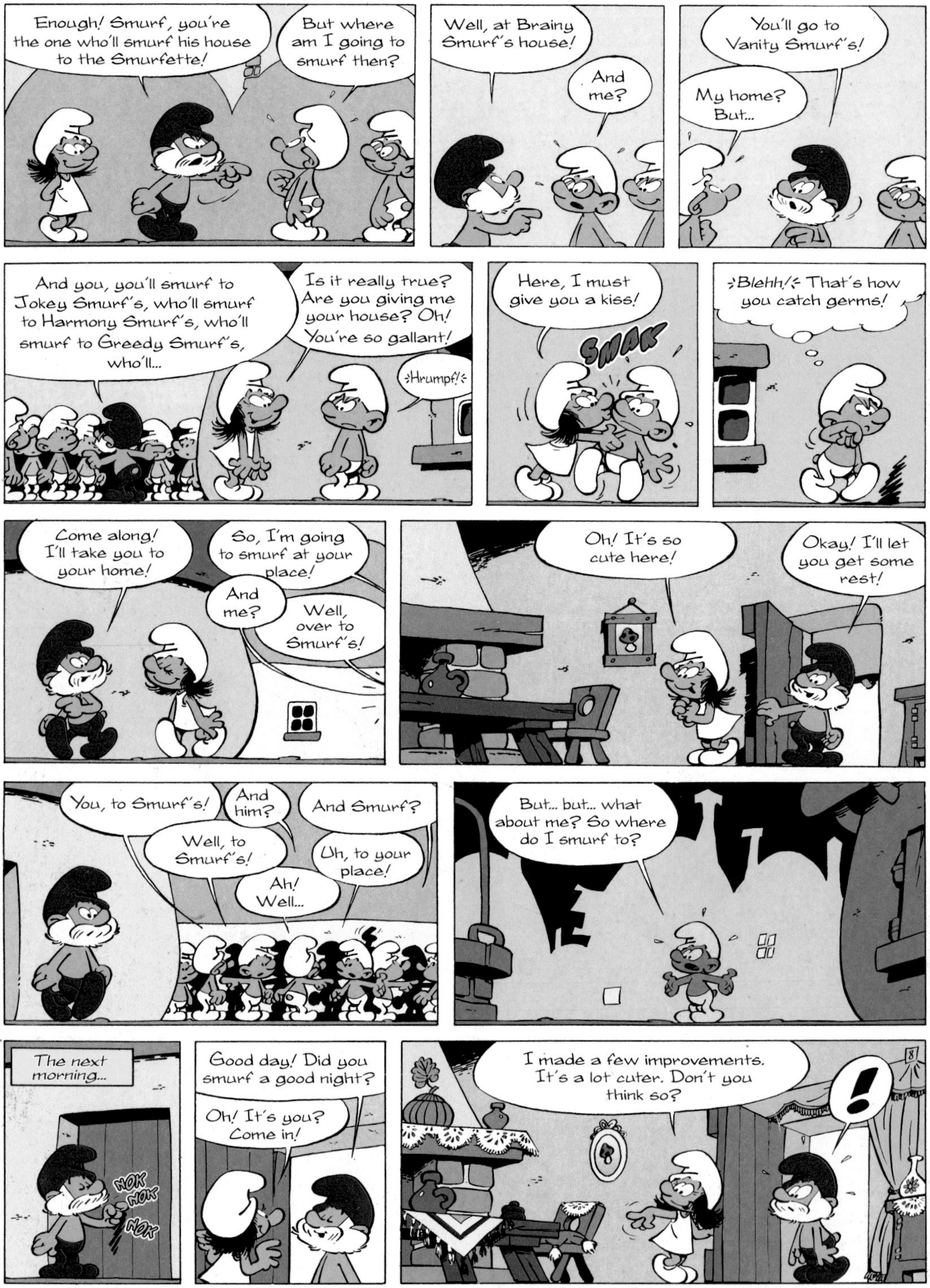
Enough! Smurf, you're the one who'll smurf his house to the Smurfette!
But where am I going to smurf then?
Well, at Brainy Smurf's house!
And me?
You'll go to Vanity Smurf's!
My home? But...
And you, you'll smurf to Jokey Smurf's, who'll smurf to Harmony Smurf's, who'll smurf to Greedy Smurf's, who'll...
Is it really true? Are you giving me your house? Oh! You're so gallant!
Hrumpf!
Here, I must give you a kiss!
SMAK
Blehh! That's how you catch germs!
Come along! I'll take you to your home!
So, I'm going to smurf at your place!
And me?
Well, over to Smurf's!
Oh! It's so cute here!
Okay! I'll let you get some rest!
You, to Smurf's!
And him?
And Smurf?
Well, to Smurf's!
Uh, to your place!
Ah! Well...
But... but... what about me? So where do I smurf to?
The next morning...
NOK NOK NOK
Good day! Did you smurf a good night?
Oh! It's you? Come in!
I made a few improvements. It's a lot cuter. Don't you think so?
!

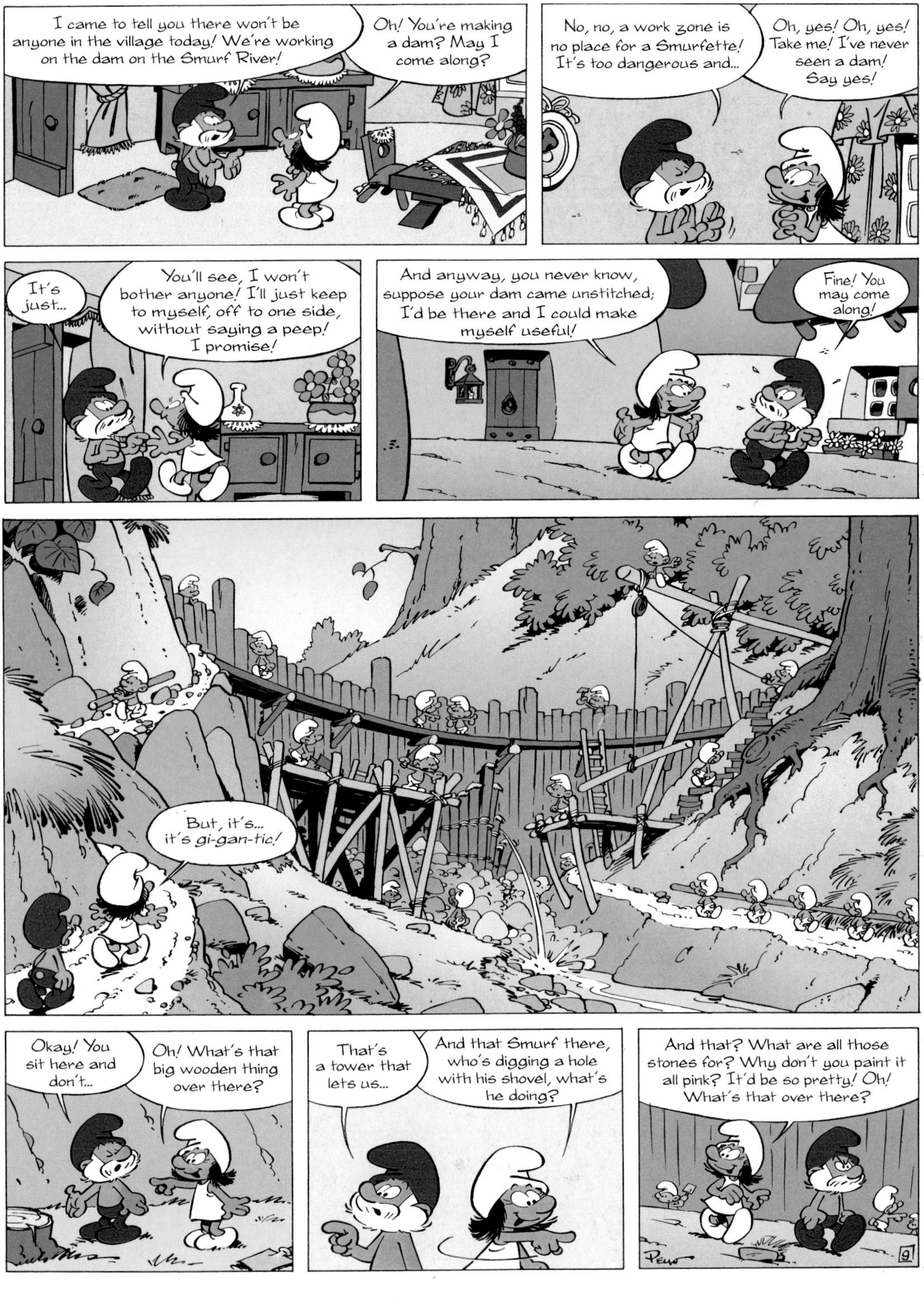

I came to tell you there won't be anyone in the village today! We're working on the dam on the Smurf River!
Oh! You're making a dam? May I come along?
No, no, a work zone is no place for a Smurfette! It's too dangerous and...
Oh, yes! Oh, yes! Take me! I've never seen a dam! Say yes!
It's just...
You'll see, I won't bother anyone! I'll just keep to myself, off to one side, without saying a peep! I promise!
And anyway, you never know, suppose your dam came unstitched; I'd be there and I could make myself useful!
Fine! You may come along!
But, it's... it's gi-gan-tic!
Okay! You sit here and don't...
Oh! What's that big wooden thing over there?
That's a tower that lets us...
And that Smurf there, who's digging a hole with his shovel, what's he doing?
And that? What are all those stones for? Why don't you paint it all pink? It'd be so pretty! Oh! What's that over there?
Peyo
9

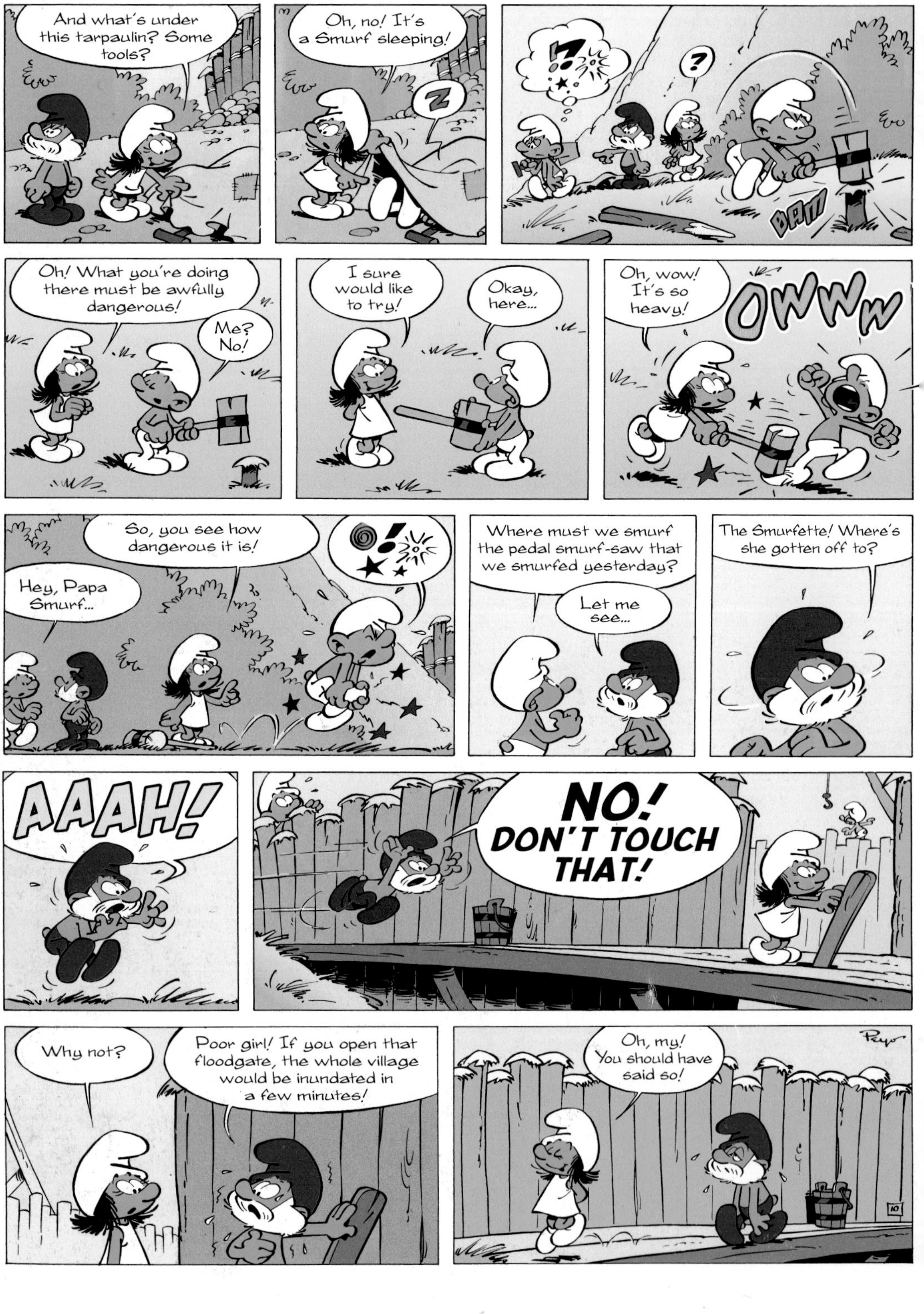
And what's under this tarpaulin? Some tools?
Oh, no! It's a Smurf sleeping!
Z
?
BAM
Oh! What you're doing there must be awfully dangerous!
Me? No!
I sure would like to try!
Okay, here...
Oh, wow! It's so heavy!
OWWW
So, you see how dangerous it is!
Hey, Papa Smurf...
Where must we smurf the pedal smurf-saw that we smurfed yesterday?
Let me see...
The Smurfette! Where's she gotten off to?
AAAH!
NO! DON'T TOUCH THAT!
Why not?
Poor girl! If you open that floodgate, the whole village would be inundated in a few minutes!
Oh, my! You should have said so!
Peyo
10

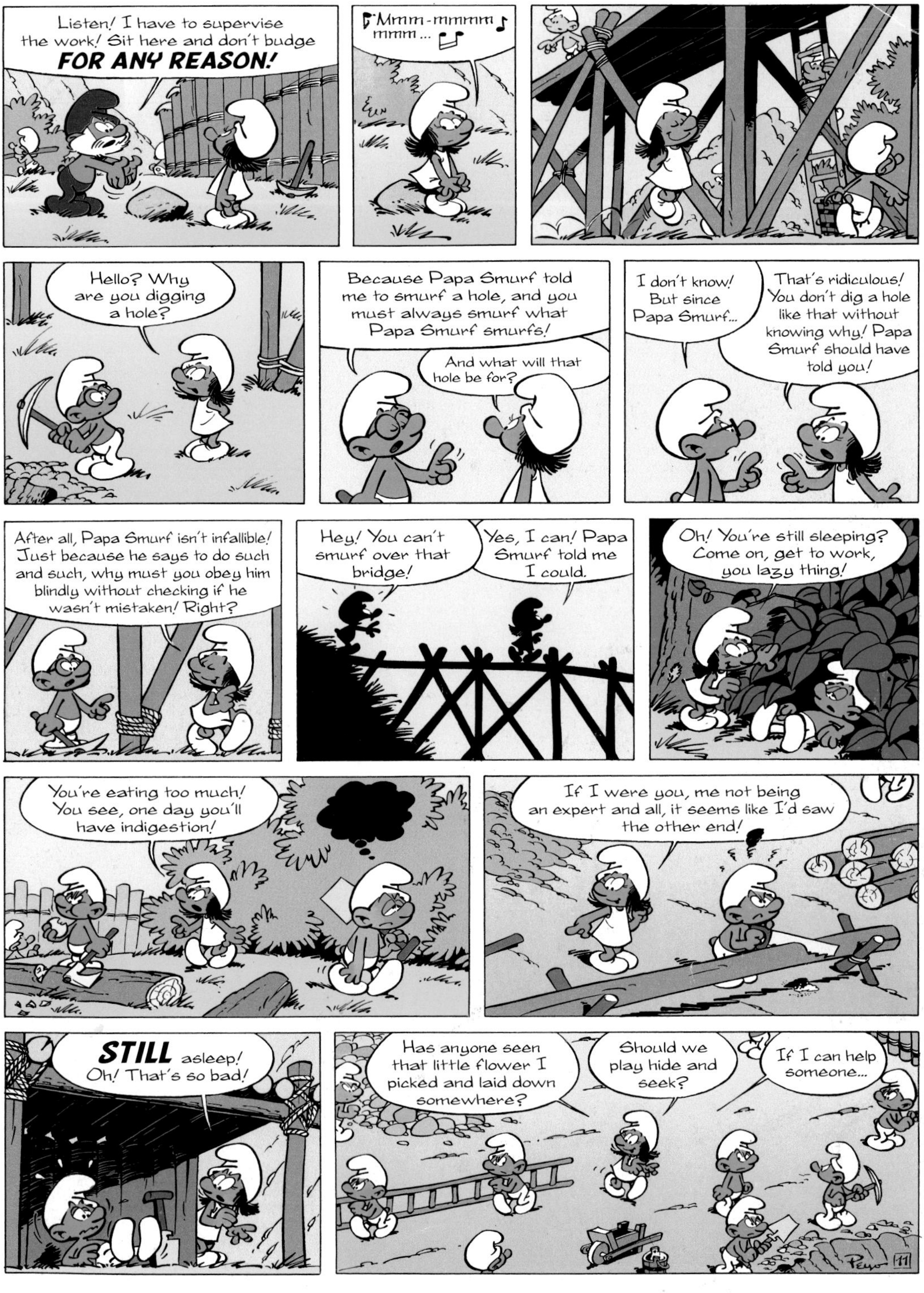

Listen! I have to supervise the work! Sit here and don't budge **FOR ANY REASON!**
Mmm-mmmm mmm...
Hello? Why are you digging a hole?
Because Papa Smurf told me to smurf a hole, and you must always smurf what Papa Smurf smurfs!
And what will that hole be for?
I don't know! But since Papa Smurf...
That's ridiculous! You don't dig a hole like that without knowing why! Papa Smurf should have told you!
After all, Papa Smurf isn't infallible! Just because he says to do such and such, why must you obey him blindly without checking if he wasn't mistaken! Right?
Hey! You can't smurf over that bridge!
Yes, I can! Papa Smurf told me I could.
Oh! You're still sleeping? Come on, get to work, you lazy thing!
You're eating too much! You see, one day you'll have indigestion!
If I were you, me not being an expert and all, it seems like I'd saw the other end!
STILL asleep! Oh! That's so bad!
Has anyone seen that little flower I picked and laid down somewhere?
Should we play hide and seek?
If I can help someone...
Peyo
11

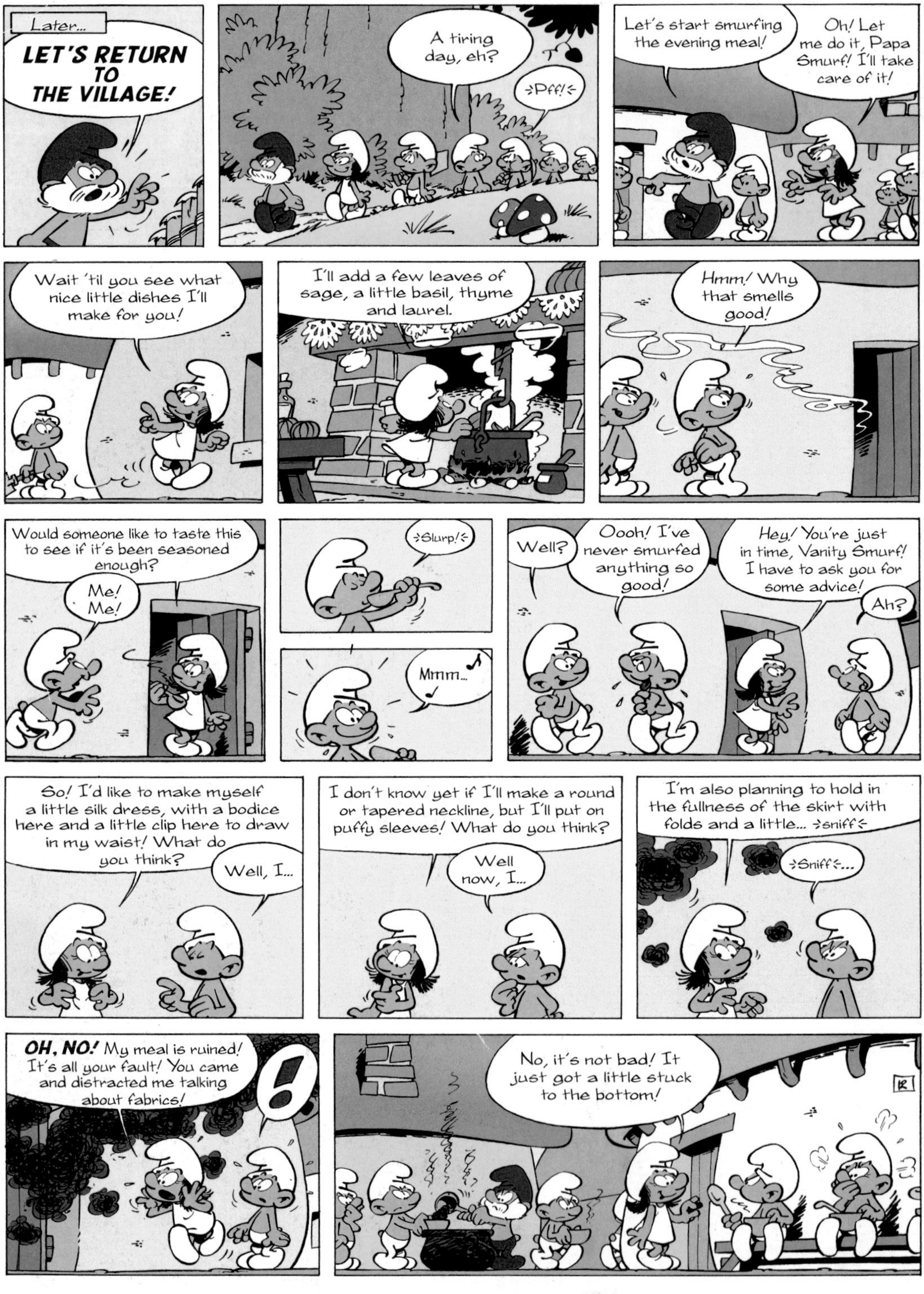
Later...
LET'S RETURN TO THE VILLAGE!
A tiring day, eh?
Pff!
Let's start smurfing the evening meal!
Oh! Let me do it, Papa Smurf! I'll take care of it!
Wait 'til you see what nice little dishes I'll make for you!
I'll add a few leaves of sage, a little basil, thyme and laurel.
Hmm! Why that smells good!
Would someone like to taste this to see if it's been seasoned enough?
Me! Me!
Slurp!
Mmm...
Well?
Oooh! I've never smurfed anything so good!
Hey! You're just in time, Vanity Smurf! I have to ask you for some advice!
Ah?
So! I'd like to make myself a little silk dress, with a bodice here and a little clip here to draw in my waist! What do you think?
Well, I...
I don't know yet if I'll make a round or tapered neckline, but I'll put on puffy sleeves! What do you think?
Well now, I...
I'm also planning to hold in the fullness of the skirt with folds and a little... sniff
Sniff...
OH, NO! My meal is ruined! It's all your fault! You came and distracted me talking about fabrics!
No, it's not bad! It just got a little stuck to the bottom!

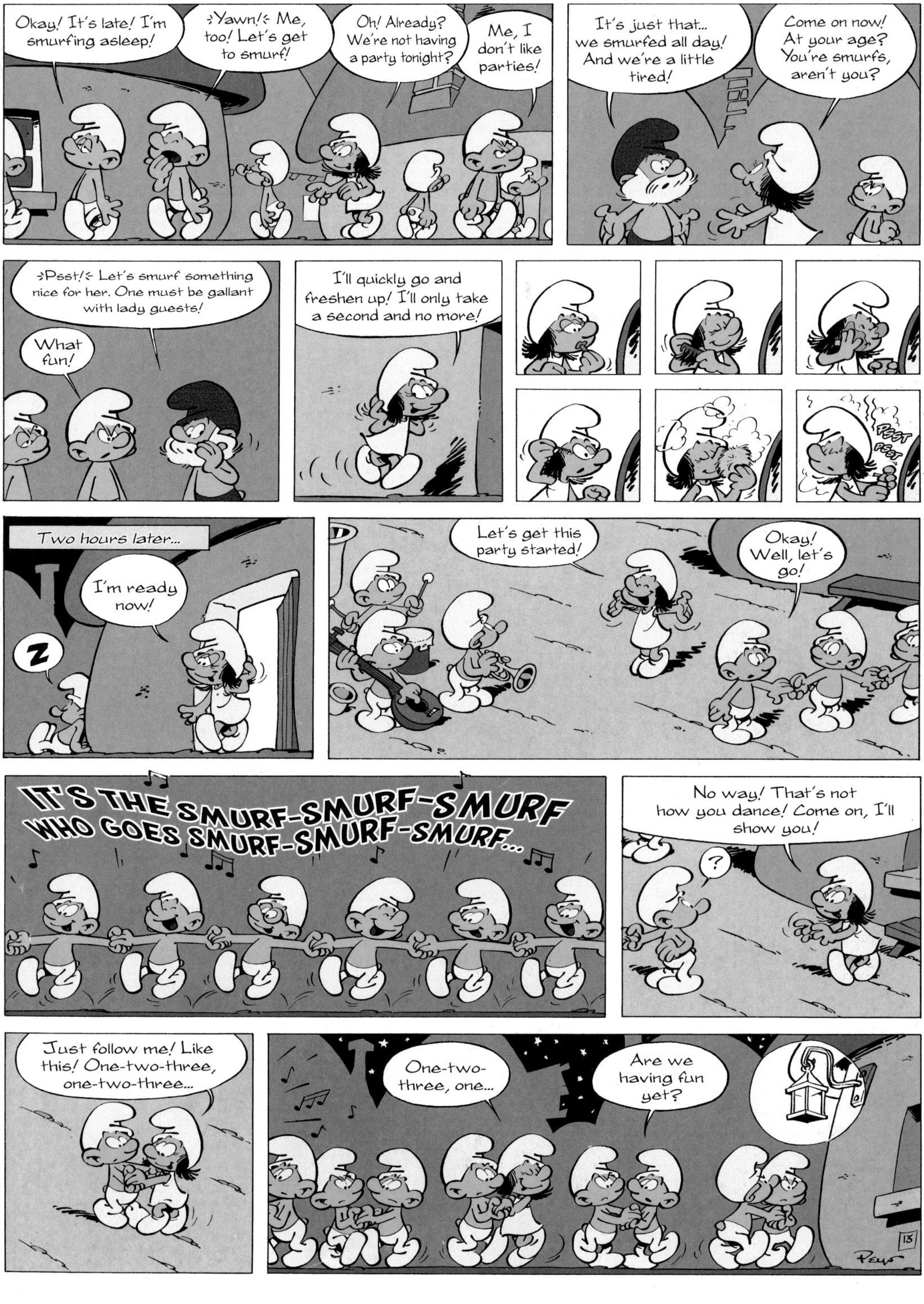
Okay! It's late! I'm smurfing asleep!
Yawn! Me, too! Let's get to smurf!
Oh! Already? We're not having a party tonight?
Me, I don't like parties!
It's just that... we smurfed all day! And we're a little tired!
Come on now! At your age? You're smurfs, aren't you?
Psst! Let's smurf something nice for her. One must be gallant with lady guests!
What fun!
I'll quickly go and freshen up! I'll only take a second and no more!
PSST
PSST
Two hours later...
I'm ready now!
Z
Let's get this party started!
Okay! Well, let's go!
IT'S THE SMURF-SMURF-SMURF WHO GOES SMURF-SMURF-SMURF...
No way! That's not how you dance! Come on, I'll show you!
?
Just follow me! Like this! One-two-three, one-two-three...
One-two-three, one...
Are we having fun yet?
13
Peyo

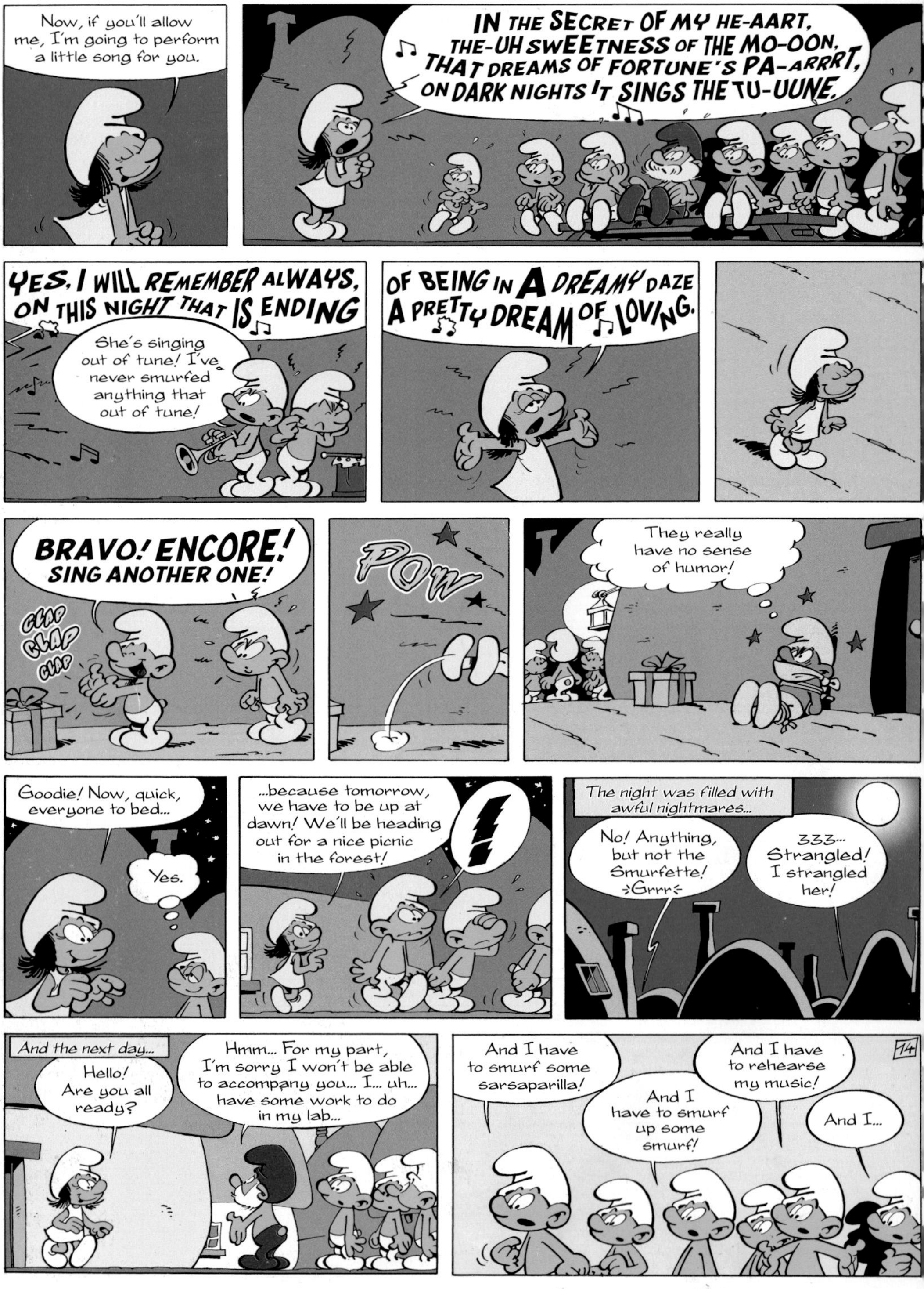
Now, if you'll allow me, I'm going to perform a little song for you.
IN THE SECRET OF MY HE-AART, THE-UH SWEETNESS OF THE MO-OON, THAT DREAMS OF FORTUNE'S PA-ARRRT, ON DARK NIGHTS IT SINGS THE TU-UUNE,
YES, I WILL REMEMBER ALWAYS, ON THIS NIGHT THAT IS ENDING
She's singing out of tune! I've never smurfed anything that out of tune!
OF BEING IN A DREAMY DAZE A PRETTY DREAM OF LOVING.
BRAVO! ENCORE! SING ANOTHER ONE!
CLAP CLAP CLAP
POW
They really have no sense of humor!
Goodie! Now, quick, everyone to bed...
Yes.
...because tomorrow, we have to be up at dawn! We'll be heading out for a nice picnic in the forest!
The night was filled with awful nightmares...
No! Anything, but not the Smurfette! Grrr
333... Strangled! I strangled her!
And the next day...
Hello! Are you all ready?
Hmm... For my part, I'm sorry I won't be able to accompany you... I... uh... have some work to do in my lab...
And I have to smurf some sarsaparilla!
And I have to smurf up some smurf!
And I have to rehearse my music!
And I...
14

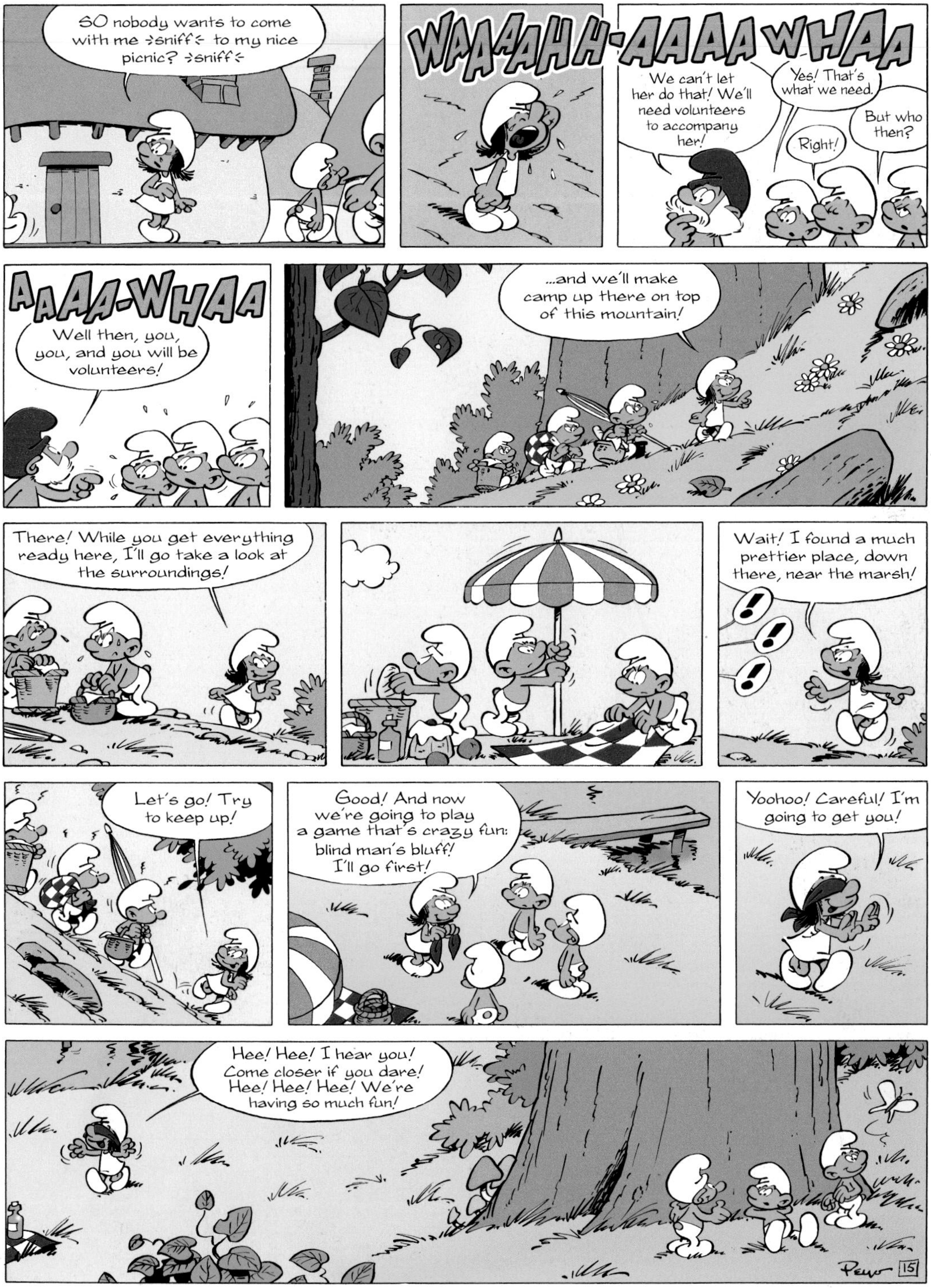

SO nobody wants to come with me >sniff< to my nice picnic? >sniff<
WAAAAHH-AAAAWHAA
We can't let her do that! We'll need volunteers to accompany her!
Yes! That's what we need.
Right!
But who then?
AAAA-WHAA
Well then, you, you, and you will be volunteers!
...and we'll make camp up there on top of this mountain!
There! While you get everything ready here, I'll go take a look at the surroundings!
Wait! I found a much prettier place, down there, near the marsh!
Let's go! Try to keep up!
Good! And now we're going to play a game that's crazy fun: blind man's bluff! I'll go first!
Yoohoo! Careful! I'm going to get you!
Hee! Hee! I hear you! Come closer if you dare! Hee! Hee! Hee! We're having so much fun!
Peyo 15

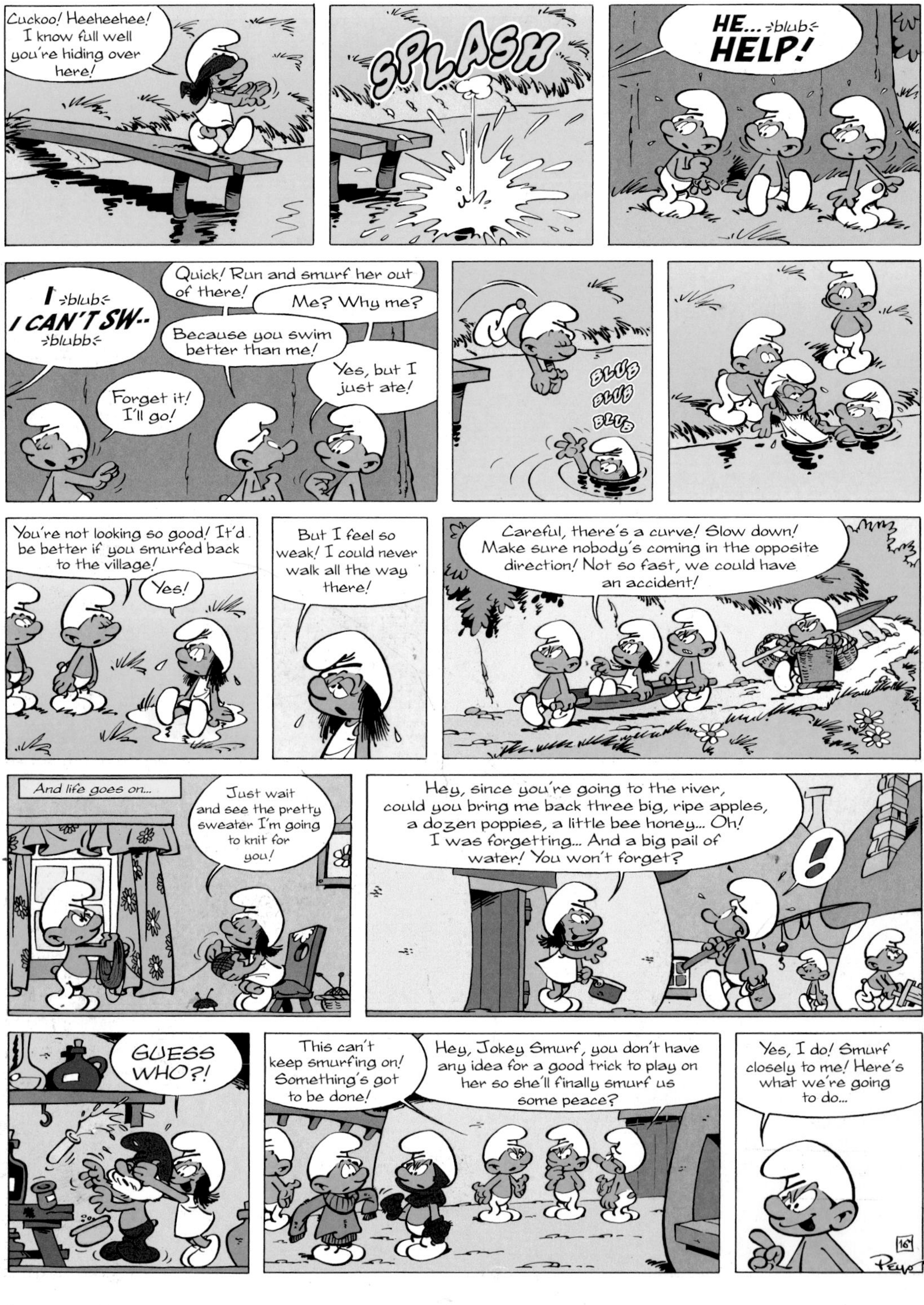

Cuckoo! Heeheehee! I know full well you're hiding over here!
SPLASH
HE... blub HELP!
I blub I CAN'T SW-- blubb
Quick! Run and smurf her out of there!
Me? Why me?
Because you swim better than me!
Yes, but I just ate!
Forget it! I'll go!
BLUB BLUB BLUB
You're not looking so good! It'd be better if you smurfed back to the village!
Yes!
But I feel so weak! I could never walk all the way there!
Careful, there's a curve! Slow down! Make sure nobody's coming in the opposite direction! Not so fast, we could have an accident!
And life goes on...
Just wait and see the pretty sweater I'm going to knit for you!
Hey, since you're going to the river, could you bring me back three big, ripe apples, a dozen poppies, a little bee honey... Oh! I was forgetting... And a big pail of water! You won't forget?
!
GUESS WHO?!
This can't keep smurfing on! Something's got to be done!
Hey, Jokey Smurf, you don't have any idea for a good trick to play on her so she'll finally smurf us some peace?
Yes, I do! Smurf closely to me! Here's what we're going to do...

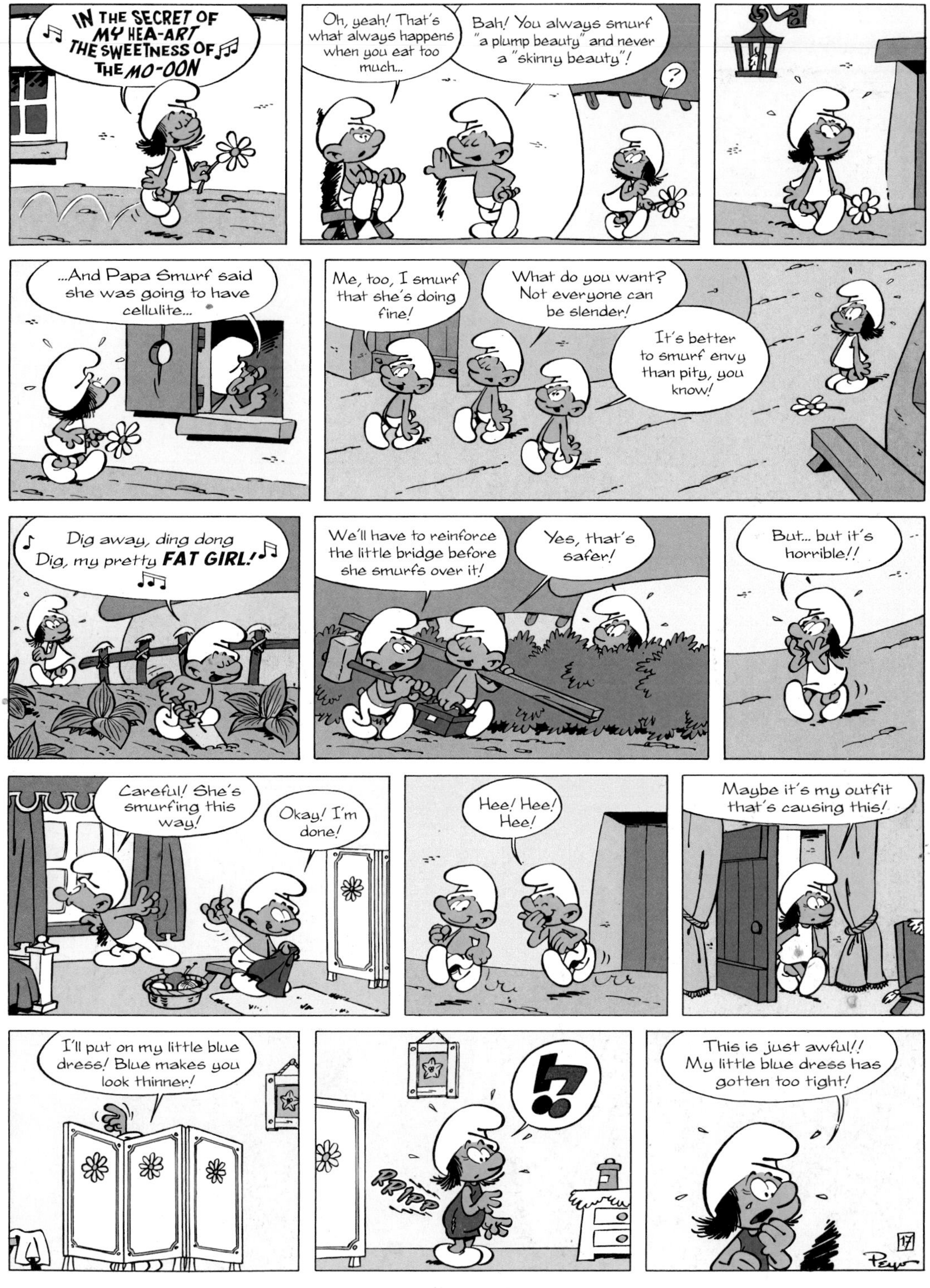
IN THE SECRET OF MY HEA-ART THE SWEETNESS OF THE MO-OON
Oh, yeah! That's what always happens when you eat too much...
Bah! You always smurf "a plump beauty" and never a "skinny beauty"!
?
...And Papa Smurf said she was going to have cellulite...
Me, too, I smurf that she's doing fine!
What do you want? Not everyone can be slender!
It's better to smurf envy than pity, you know!
Dig away, ding dong Dig, my pretty FAT GIRL!
We'll have to reinforce the little bridge before she smurfs over it!
Yes, that's safer!
But... but it's horrible!!
Careful! She's smurfing this way!
Okay! I'm done!
Hee! Hee! Hee!
Maybe it's my outfit that's causing this!
I'll put on my little blue dress! Blue makes you look thinner!
RRIPP
This is just awful!! My little blue dress has gotten too tight!
17
Peyo

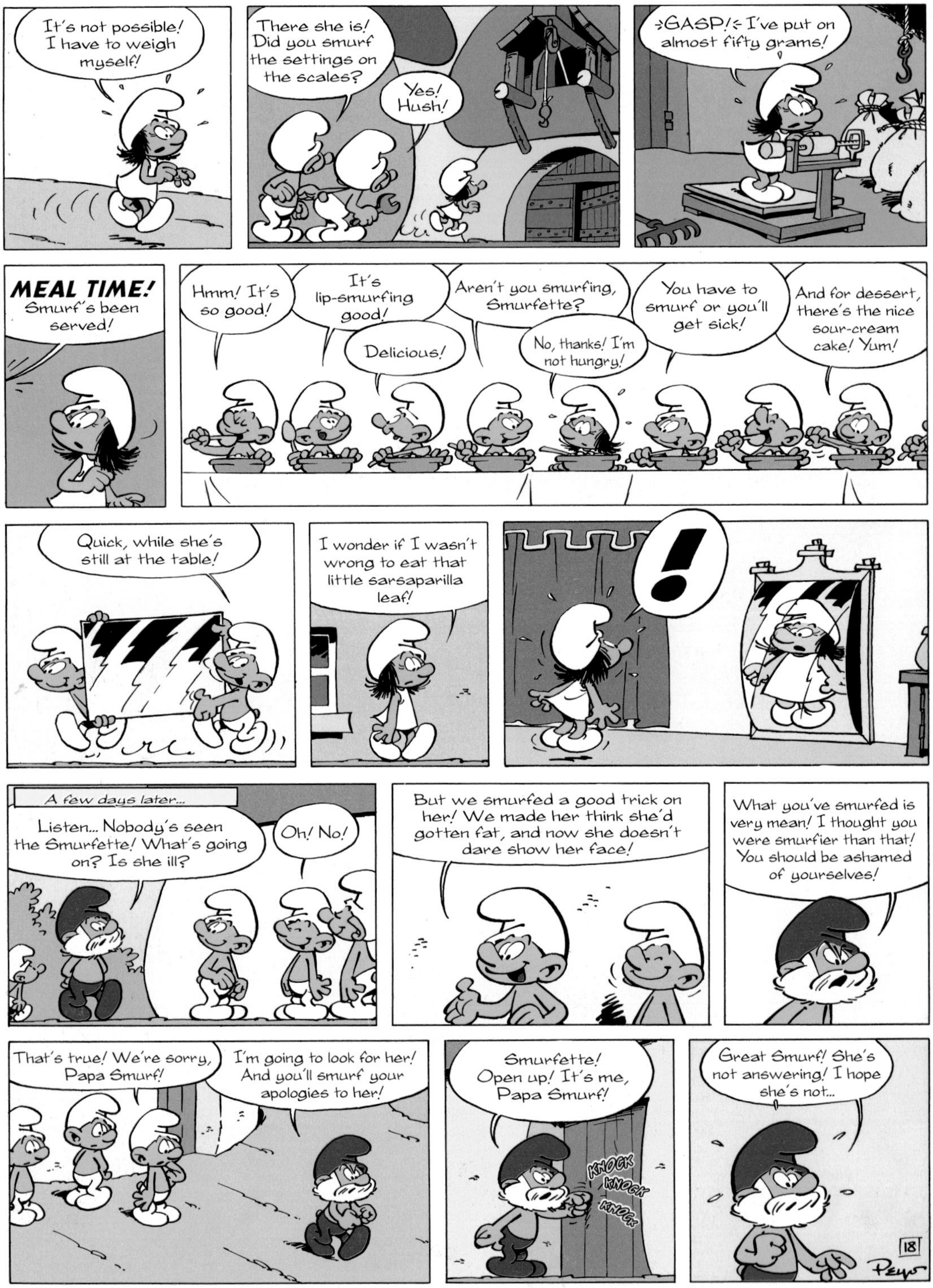

It's not possible! I have to weigh myself!
There she is! Did you smurf the settings on the scales?
Yes! Hush!
GASP! I've put on almost fifty grams!
MEAL TIME! Smurf's been served!
Hmm! It's so good!
It's lip-smurfing good!
Delicious!
Aren't you smurfing, Smurfette?
No, thanks! I'm not hungry!
You have to smurf or you'll get sick!
And for dessert, there's the nice sour-cream cake! Yum!
Quick, while she's still at the table!
I wonder if I wasn't wrong to eat that little sarsaparilla leaf!
!
A few days later...
Listen... Nobody's seen the Smurfette! What's going on? Is she ill?
Oh! No!
But we smurfed a good trick on her! We made her think she'd gotten fat, and now she doesn't dare show her face!
What you've smurfed is very mean! I thought you were smurfier than that! You should be ashamed of yourselves!
That's true! We're sorry, Papa Smurf!
I'm going to look for her! And you'll smurf your apologies to her!
Smurfette! Open up! It's me, Papa Smurf!
KNOCK KNOCK KNOCK
Great Smurf! She's not answering! I hope she's not...
18
Peyo

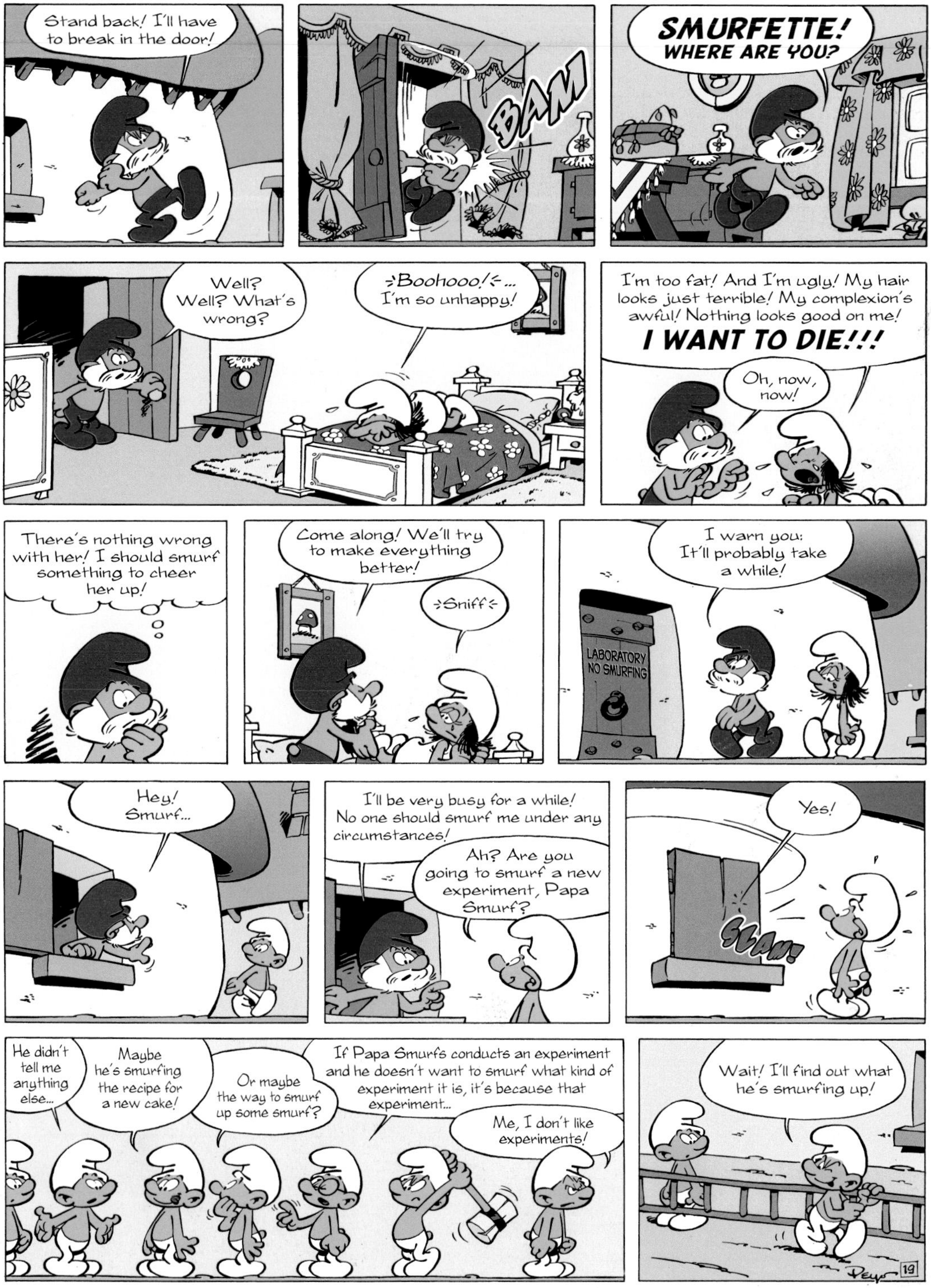
Stand back! I'll have to break in the door!
BAM
SMURFETTE! WHERE ARE YOU?
Well? Well? What's wrong?
Boohooo!... I'm so unhappy!
I'm too fat! And I'm ugly! My hair looks just terrible! My complexion's awful! Nothing looks good on me! I WANT TO DIE!!!
Oh, now, now!
There's nothing wrong with her! I should smurf something to cheer her up!
Come along! We'll try to make everything better!
Sniff
I warn you: It'll probably take a while!
LABORATORY NO SMURFING
Hey! Smurf...
I'll be very busy for a while! No one should smurf me under any circumstances!
Ah? Are you going to smurf a new experiment, Papa Smurf?
Yes!
SLAM!
He didn't tell me anything else...
Maybe he's smurfing the recipe for a new cake!
Or maybe the way to smurf up some smurf?
If Papa Smurfs conducts an experiment and he doesn't want to smurf what kind of experiment it is, it's because that experiment...
Me, I don't like experiments!
Wait! I'll find out what he's smurfing up!
Peyo
19

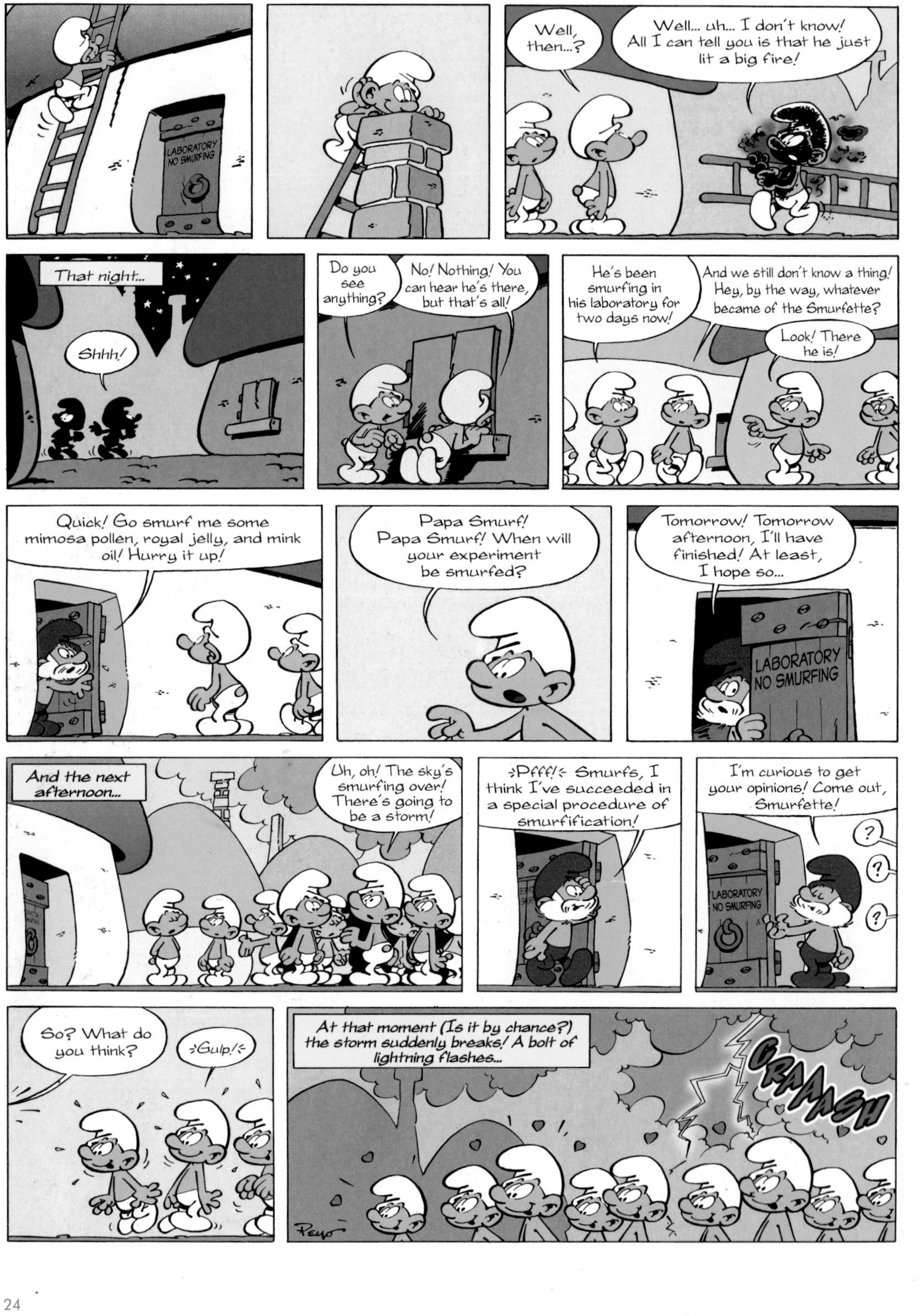

LABORATORY NO SMURFING
Well, then...?
Well... uh... I don't know! All I can tell you is that he just lit a big fire!
That night...
Shhh!
Do you see anything?
No! Nothing! You can hear he's there, but that's all!
He's been smurfing in his laboratory for two days now!
And we still don't know a thing! Hey, by the way, whatever became of the Smurfette?
Look! There he is!
Quick! Go smurf me some mimosa pollen, royal jelly, and mink oil! Hurry it up!
Papa Smurf! Papa Smurf! When will your experiment be smurfed?
Tomorrow! Tomorrow afternoon, I'll have finished! At least, I hope so...
LABORATORY NO SMURFING
And the next afternoon...
Uh, oh! The sky's smurfing over! There's going to be a storm!
Pfff! Smurfs, I think I've succeeded in a special procedure of smurfification!
I'm curious to get your opinions! Come out, Smurfette!
LABORATORY NO SMURFING
?
?
?
So? What do you think?
Gulp!
At that moment (Is it by chance?) the storm suddenly breaks! A bolt of lightning flashes...
CRAAASH

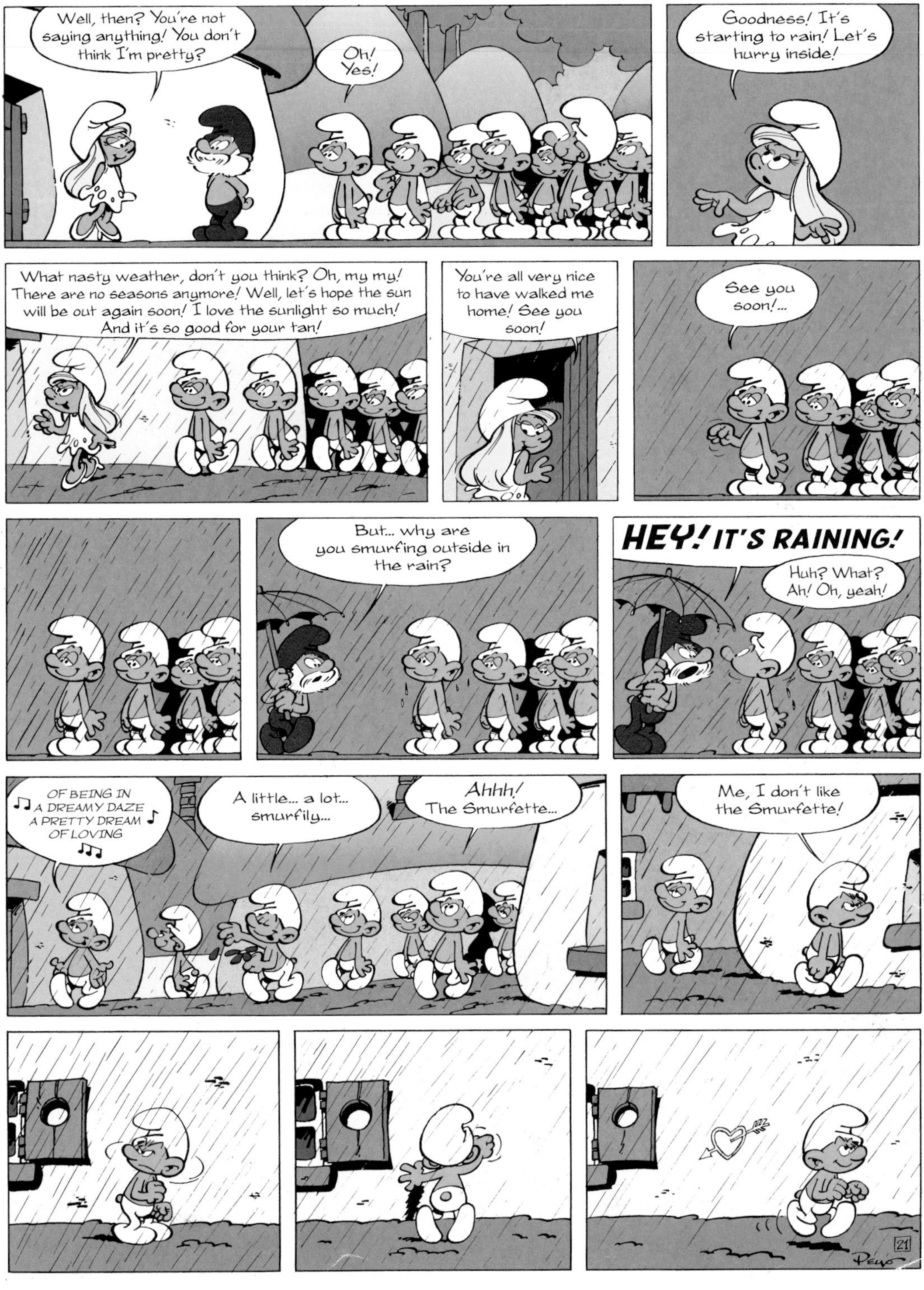
Well, then? You're not saying anything! You don't think I'm pretty?
Oh! Yes!
Goodness! It's starting to rain! Let's hurry inside!
What nasty weather, don't you think? Oh, my my! There are no seasons anymore! Well, let's hope the sun will be out again soon! I love the sunlight so much! And it's so good for your tan!
You're all very nice to have walked me home! See you soon!
See you soon!...
But... why are you smurfing outside in the rain?
HEY! IT'S RAINING!
Huh? What? Ah! Oh, yeah!
OF BEING IN A DREAMY DAZE A PRETTY DREAM OF LOVING
A little... a lot... smurfily...
Ahhh! The Smurfette...
Me, I don't like the Smurfette!
21
PEYO

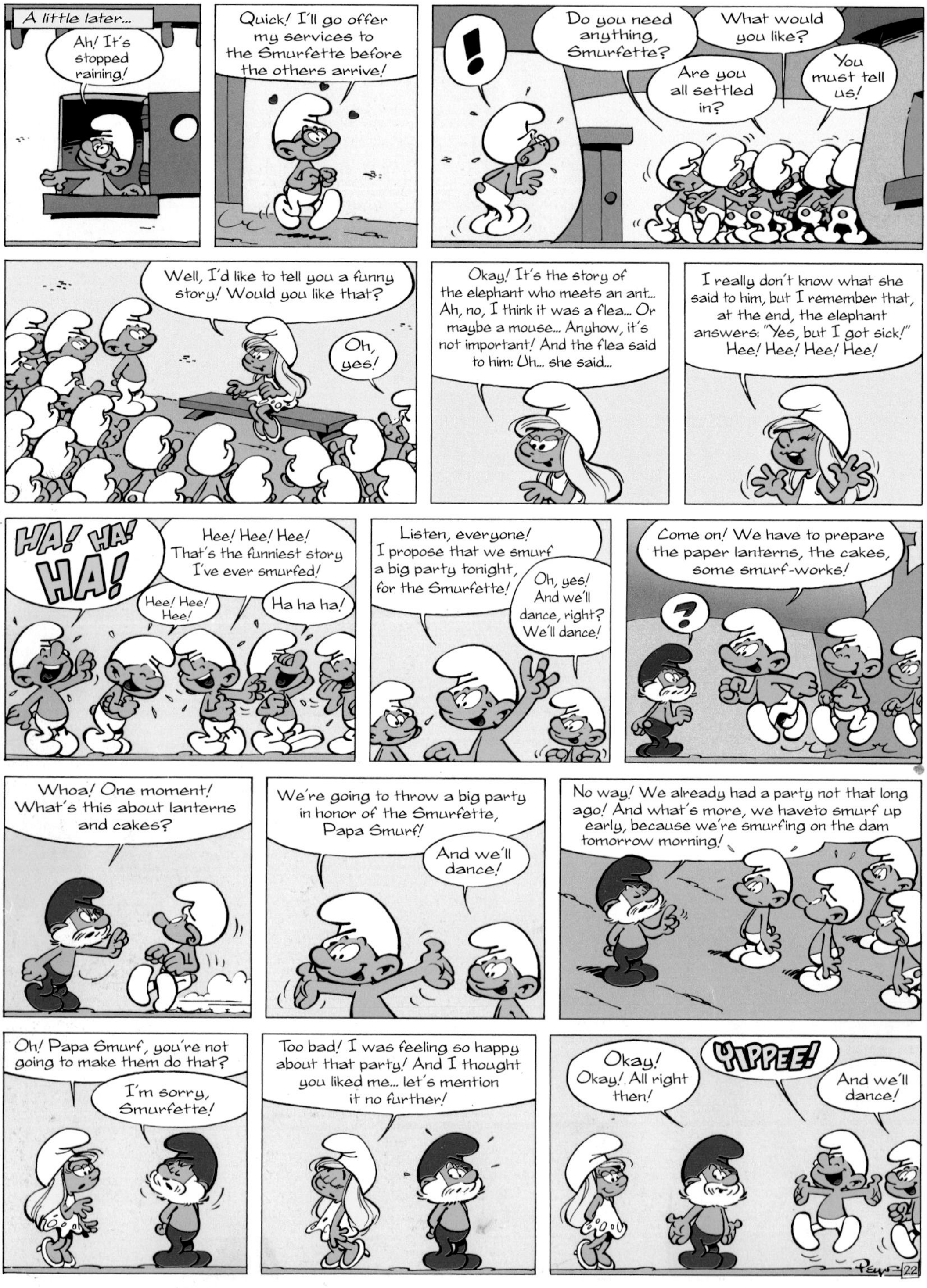
A little later...
Ah! It's stopped raining!
Quick! I'll go offer my services to the Smurfette before the others arrive!
!
Do you need anything, Smurfette?
What would you like?
Are you all settled in?
You must tell us!
Well, I'd like to tell you a funny story! Would you like that?
Oh, yes!
Okay! It's the story of the elephant who meets an ant... Ah, no, I think it was a flea... Or maybe a mouse... Anyhow, it's not important! And the flea said to him: Uh... she said...
I really don't know what she said to him, but I remember that, at the end, the elephant answers: "Yes, but I got sick!" Hee! Hee! Hee! Hee!
HA! HA! HA!
Hee! Hee! Hee! That's the funniest story I've ever smurfed!
Hee! Hee! Hee!
Ha ha ha!
Listen, everyone! I propose that we smurf a big party tonight, for the Smurfette!
Oh, yes! And we'll dance, right? We'll dance!
Come on! We have to prepare the paper lanterns, the cakes, some smurf-works!
?
Whoa! One moment! What's this about lanterns and cakes?
We're going to throw a big party in honor of the Smurfette, Papa Smurf!
And we'll dance!
No way! We already had a party not that long ago! And what's more, we haveto smurf up early, because we're smurfing on the dam tomorrow morning!
Oh! Papa Smurf, you're not going to make them do that?
I'm sorry, Smurfette!
Too bad! I was feeling so happy about that party! And I thought you liked me... let's mention it no further!
Okay! Okay! All right then!
YIPPEE!
And we'll dance!
Peyo 22

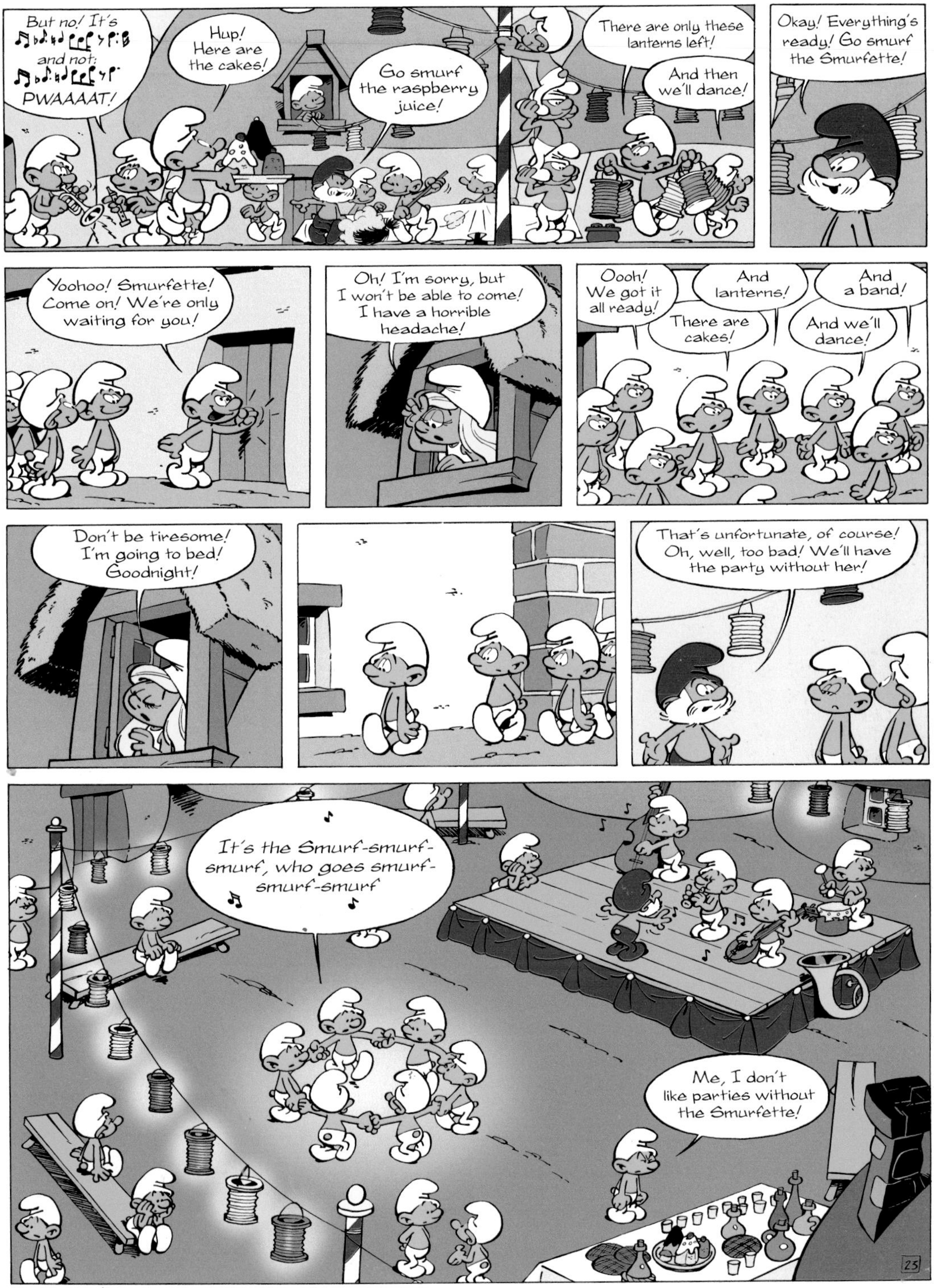

But no! It's ♫♩♩♩ and not: ♫♩♩♩ PWAAAAT!
Hup! Here are the cakes!
Go smurf the raspberry juice!
There are only these lanterns left!
And then we'll dance!
Okay! Everything's ready! Go smurf the Smurfette!
Yoohoo! Smurfette! Come on! We're only waiting for you!
Oh! I'm sorry, but I won't be able to come! I have a horrible headache!
Oooh! We got it all ready!
And lanterns!
There are cakes!
And a band!
And we'll dance!
Don't be tiresome! I'm going to bed! Goodnight!
That's unfortunate, of course! Oh, well, too bad! We'll have the party without her!
It's the Smurf-smurf-smurf, who goes smurf-smurf-smurf
Me, I don't like parties without the Smurfette!
23

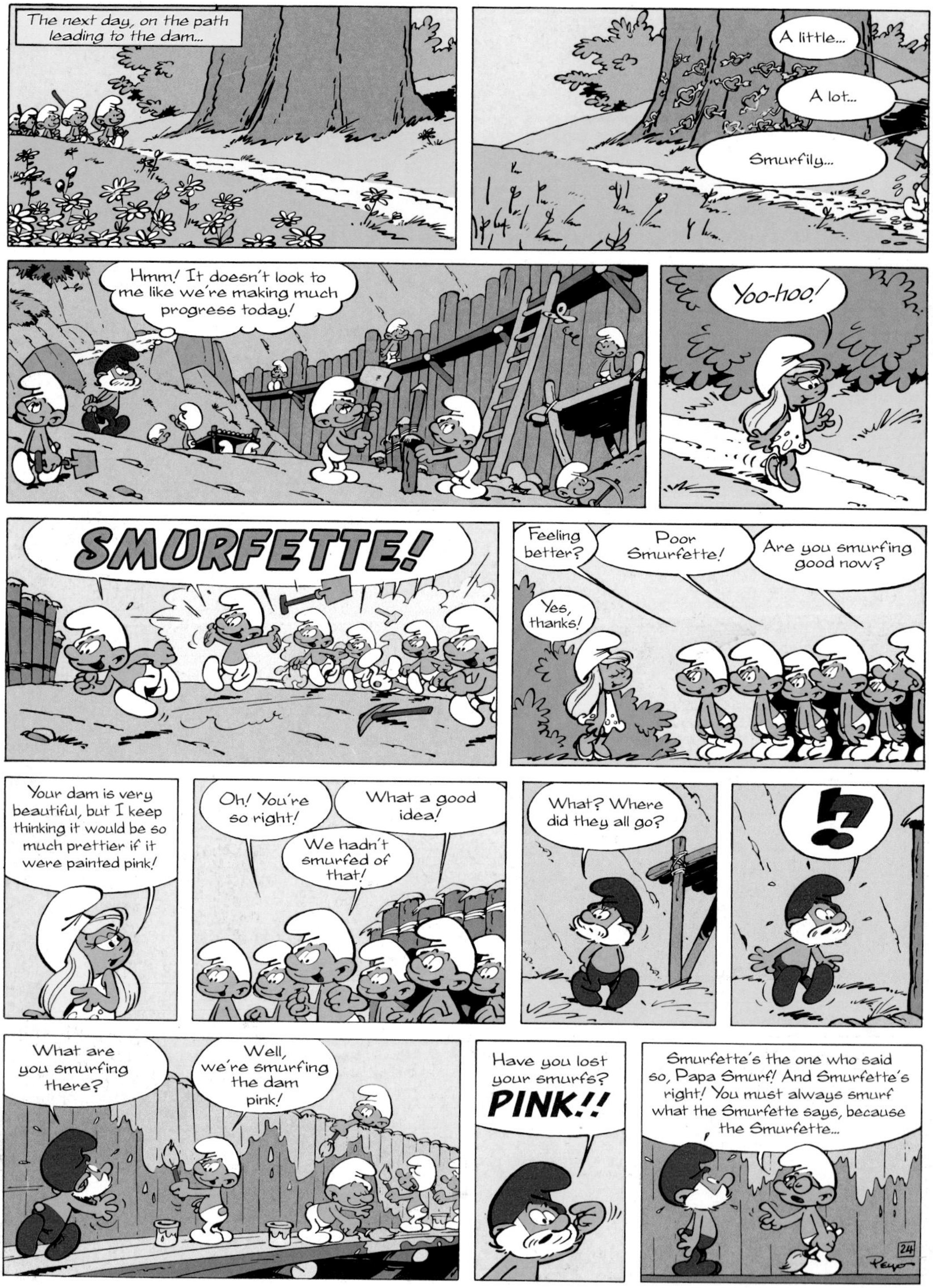
The next day, on the path leading to the dam...
A little...
A lot...
Smurfily...
Hmm! It doesn't look to me like we're making much progress today!
Yoo-hoo!
SMURFETTE!
Feeling better?
Poor Smurfette!
Are you smurfing good now?
Yes, thanks!
Your dam is very beautiful, but I keep thinking it would be so much prettier if it were painted pink!
Oh! You're so right!
What a good idea!
We hadn't smurfed of that!
What? Where did they all go?
!?
What are you smurfing there?
Well, we're smurfing the dam pink!
Have you lost your smurfs? PINK!!
Smurfette's the one who said so, Papa Smurf! And Smurfette's right! You must always smurf what the Smurfette says, because the Smurfette...
24
Peyo

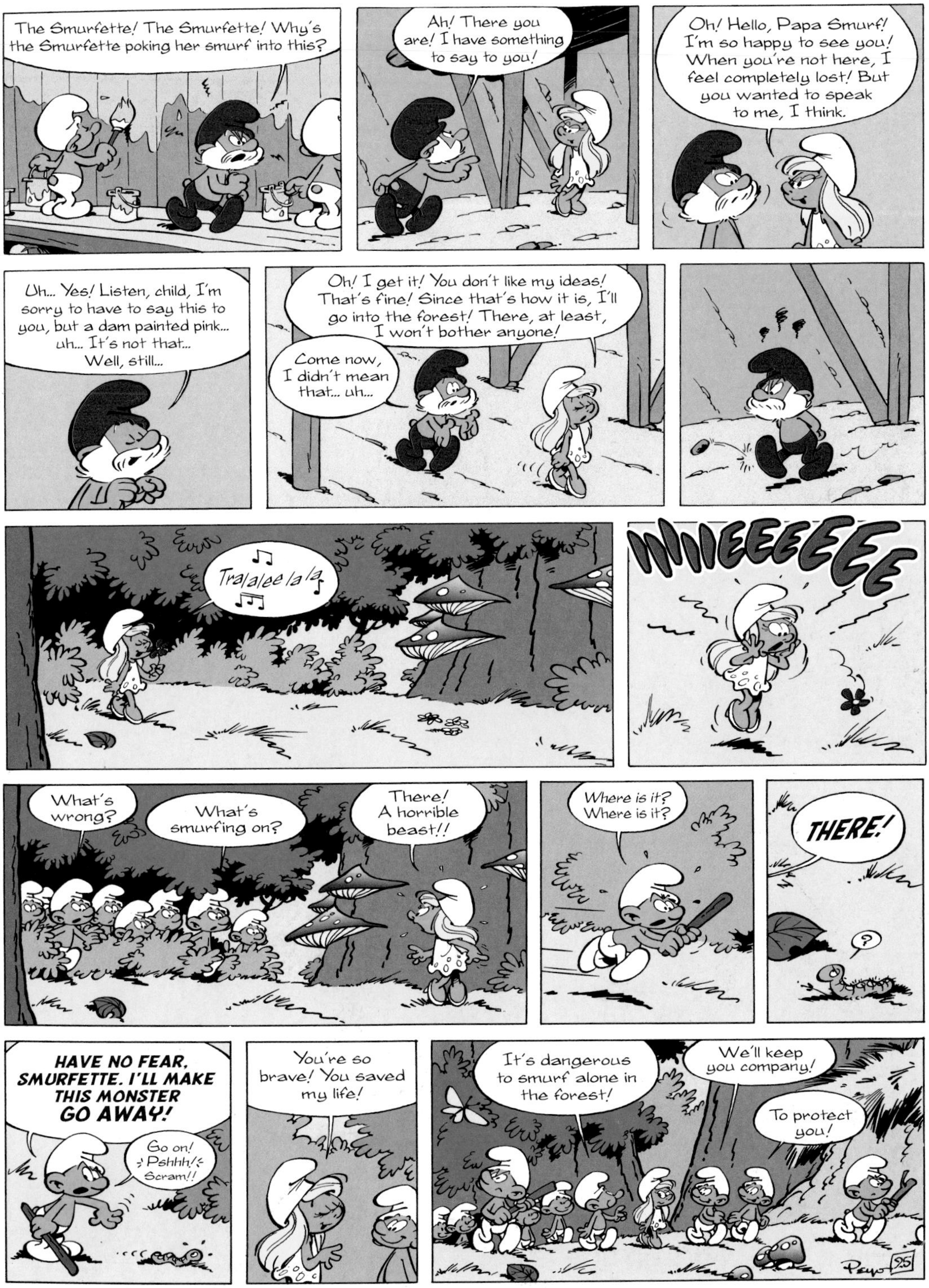
The Smurfette! The Smurfette! Why's the Smurfette poking her smurf into this?
Ah! There you are! I have something to say to you!
Oh! Hello, Papa Smurf! I'm so happy to see you! When you're not here, I feel completely lost! But you wanted to speak to me, I think.
Uh... Yes! Listen, child, I'm sorry to have to say this to you, but a dam painted pink... uh... It's not that... Well, still...
Oh! I get it! You don't like my ideas! That's fine! Since that's how it is, I'll go into the forest! There, at least, I won't bother anyone!
Come now, I didn't mean that... uh...
Tralalee la la
WIIIEEEEEEE
What's wrong?
What's smurfing on?
There! A horrible beast!!
Where is it? Where is it?
THERE!
?
HAVE NO FEAR, SMURFETTE. I'LL MAKE THIS MONSTER GO AWAY!
Go on! Pshhh! Scram!!
You're so brave! You saved my life!
It's dangerous to smurf alone in the forest!
We'll keep you company!
To protect you!
Peyo 25

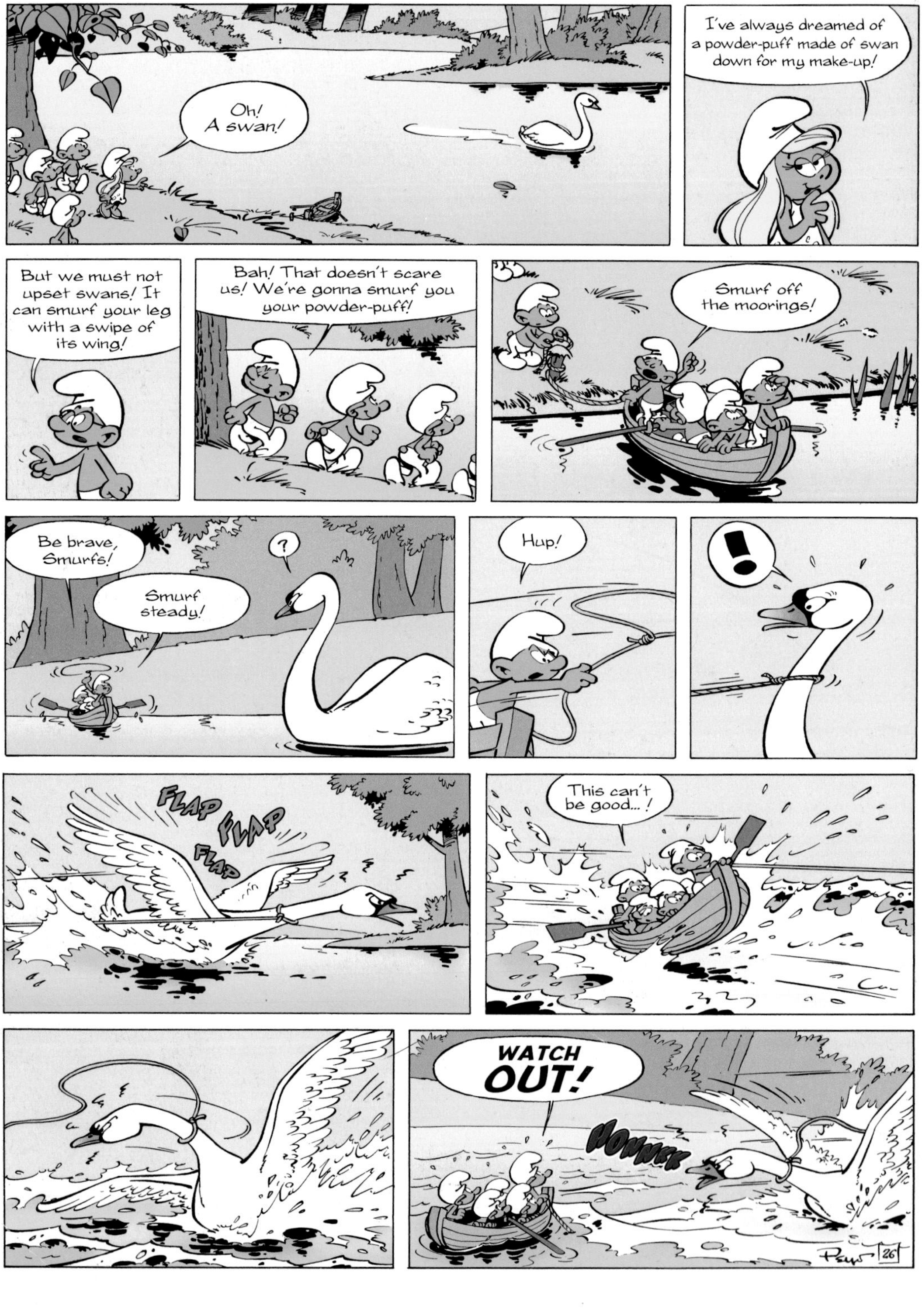
Oh! A swan!
I've always dreamed of a powder-puff made of swan down for my make-up!
But we must not upset swans! It can smurf your leg with a swipe of its wing!
Bah! That doesn't scare us! We're gonna smurf you your powder-puff!
Smurf off the moorings!
Be brave, Smurfs!
Smurf steady!
?
Hup!
!
FLAP FLAP FLAP
This can't be good... !
WATCH OUT!
HONNKK
26

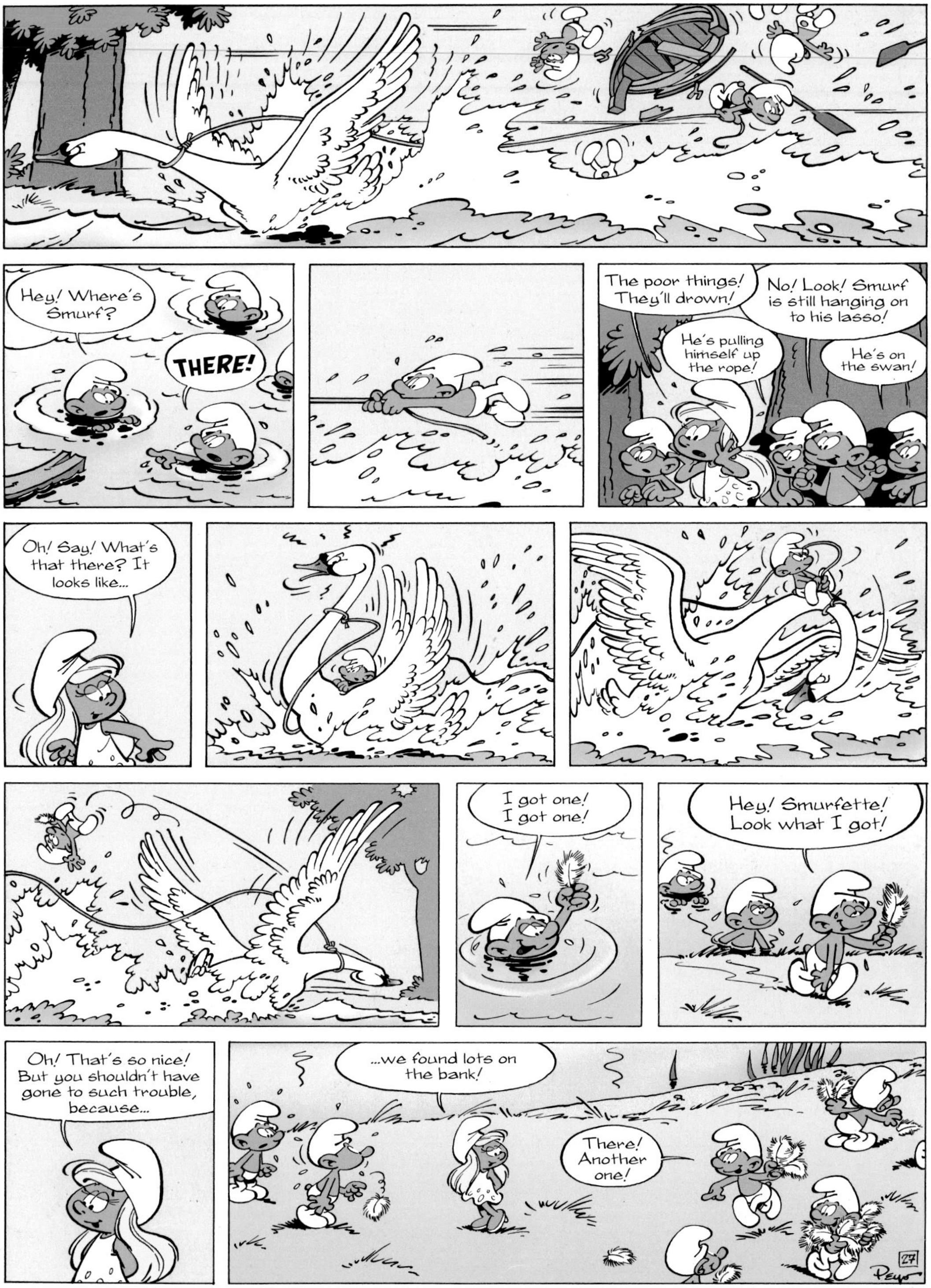

Hey! Where's Smurf?
THERE!
The poor things! They'll drown!
No! Look! Smurf is still hanging on to his lasso!
He's pulling himself up the rope!
He's on the swan!
Oh! Say! What's that there? It looks like...
I got one! I got one!
Hey! Smurfette! Look what I got!
Oh! That's so nice! But you shouldn't have gone to such trouble, because...
...we found lots on the bank!
There! Another one!
27
Peyo

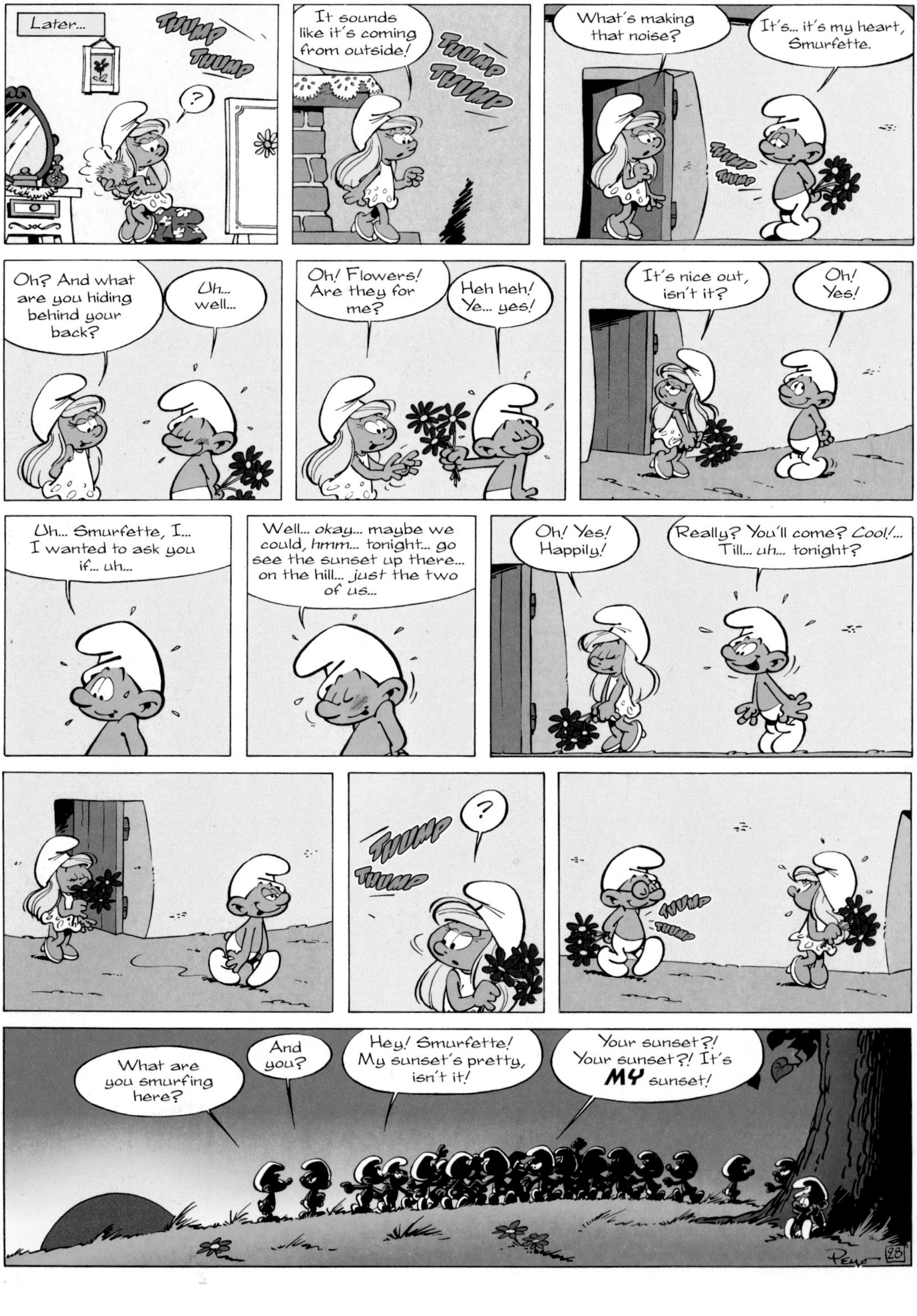
Later...
THUMP
THUMP
?
It sounds like it's coming from outside!
THUMP
THUMP
What's making that noise?
It's... it's my heart, Smurfette.
THUMP
THUMP
Oh? And what are you hiding behind your back?
Uh... well...
Oh! Flowers! Are they for me?
Heh heh! Ye... yes!
It's nice out, isn't it?
Oh! Yes!
Uh... Smurfette, I... I wanted to ask you if... uh...
Well... okay... maybe we could, hmm... tonight... go see the sunset up there... on the hill... just the two of us...
Oh! Yes! Happily!
Really? You'll come? Cool!... Till... uh... tonight?
THUMP
THUMP
?
THUMP
THUMP
What are you smurfing here?
And you?
Hey! Smurfette! My sunset's pretty, isn't it!
Your sunset?! Your sunset?! It's MY sunset!
Peyo
28

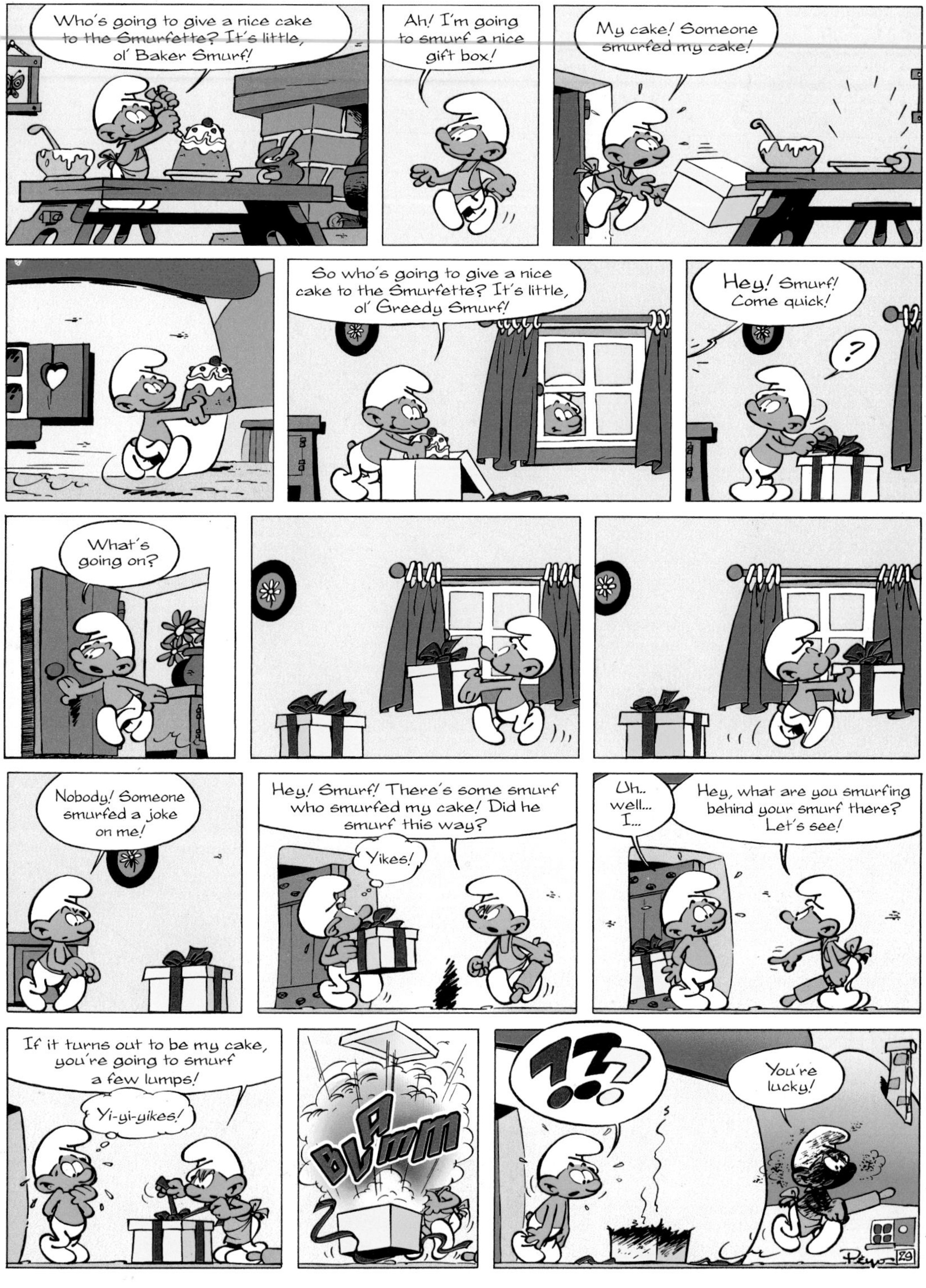

Who's going to give a nice cake to the Smurfette? It's little, ol' Baker Smurf!
Ah! I'm going to smurf a nice gift box!
My cake! Someone smurfed my cake!
So who's going to give a nice cake to the Smurfette? It's little, ol' Greedy Smurf!
Hey! Smurf! Come quick!
?
What's going on?
Nobody! Someone smurfed a joke on me!
Hey! Smurf! There's some smurf who smurfed my cake! Did he smurf this way?
Yikes!
Uh.. well... I...
Hey, what are you smurfing behind your smurf there? Let's see!
If it turns out to be my cake, you're going to smurf a few lumps!
Yi-yi-yikes!
BLAMM
??
You're lucky!

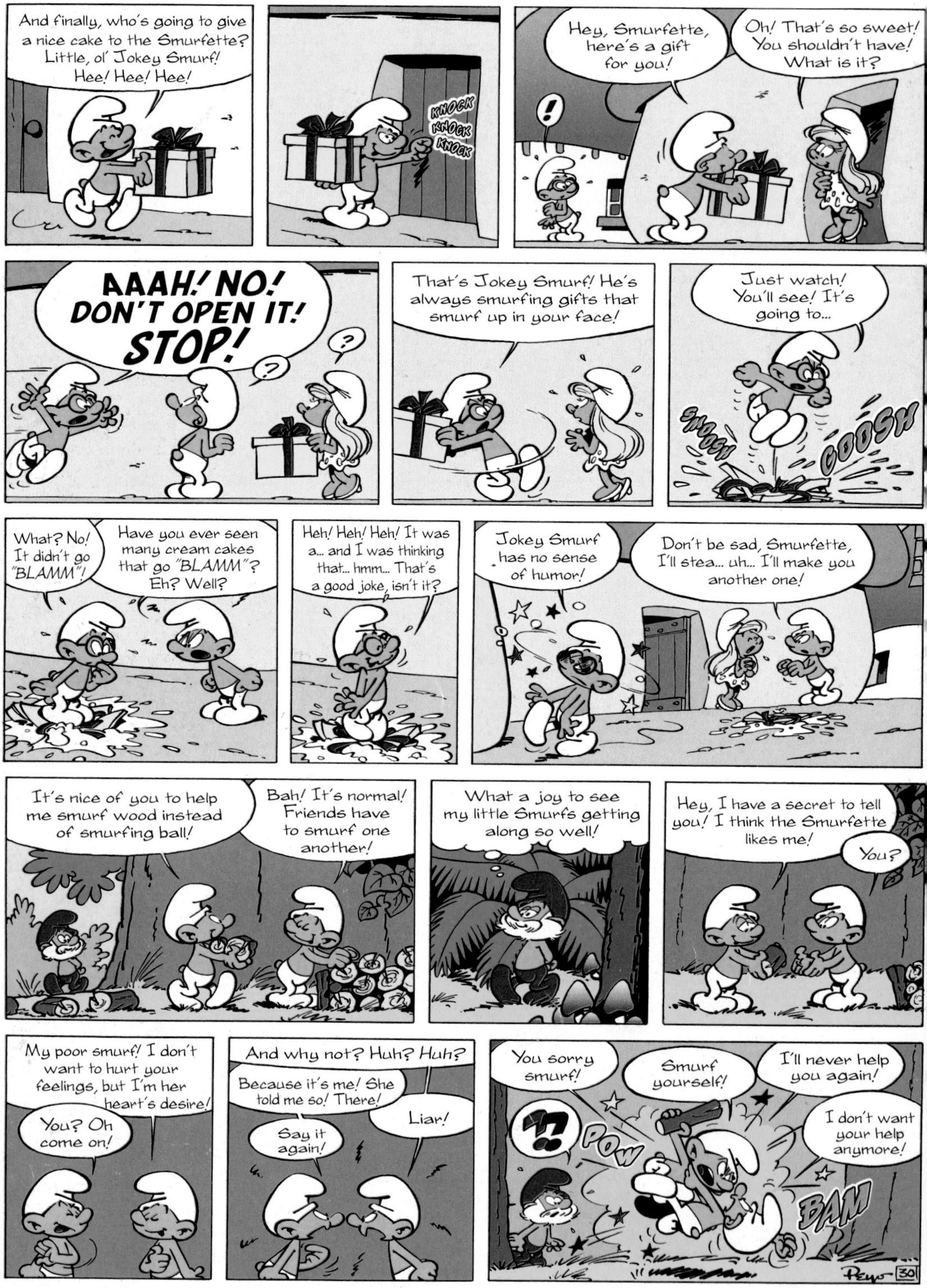
And finally, who's going to give a nice cake to the Smurfette? Little, ol' Jokey Smurf! Hee! Hee! Hee!
KNOCK KNOCK KNOCK
Hey, Smurfette, here's a gift for you!
Oh! That's so sweet! You shouldn't have! What is it?
!
AAAH! NO! DON'T OPEN IT! STOP!
?
?
That's Jokey Smurf! He's always smurfing gifts that smurf up in your face!
Just watch! You'll see! It's going to...
SWOOSH
COOSH
What? No! It didn't go "BLAMM"!
Have you ever seen many cream cakes that go "BLAMM"? Eh? Well?
Heh! Heh! Heh! It was a... and I was thinking that... hmm... That's a good joke, isn't it?
Jokey Smurf has no sense of humor!
Don't be sad, Smurfette, I'll stea... uh... I'll make you another one!
It's nice of you to help me smurf wood instead of smurfing ball!
Bah! It's normal! Friends have to smurf one another!
What a joy to see my little Smurfs getting along so well!
Hey, I have a secret to tell you! I think the Smurfette likes me!
You?
My poor smurf! I don't want to hurt your feelings, but I'm her heart's desire!
You? Oh come on!
And why not? Huh? Huh?
Because it's me! She told me so! There!
Say it again!
Liar!
You sorry smurf!
Smurf yourself!
I'll never help you again!
I don't want your help anymore!
POW
BAM
Peyo
30

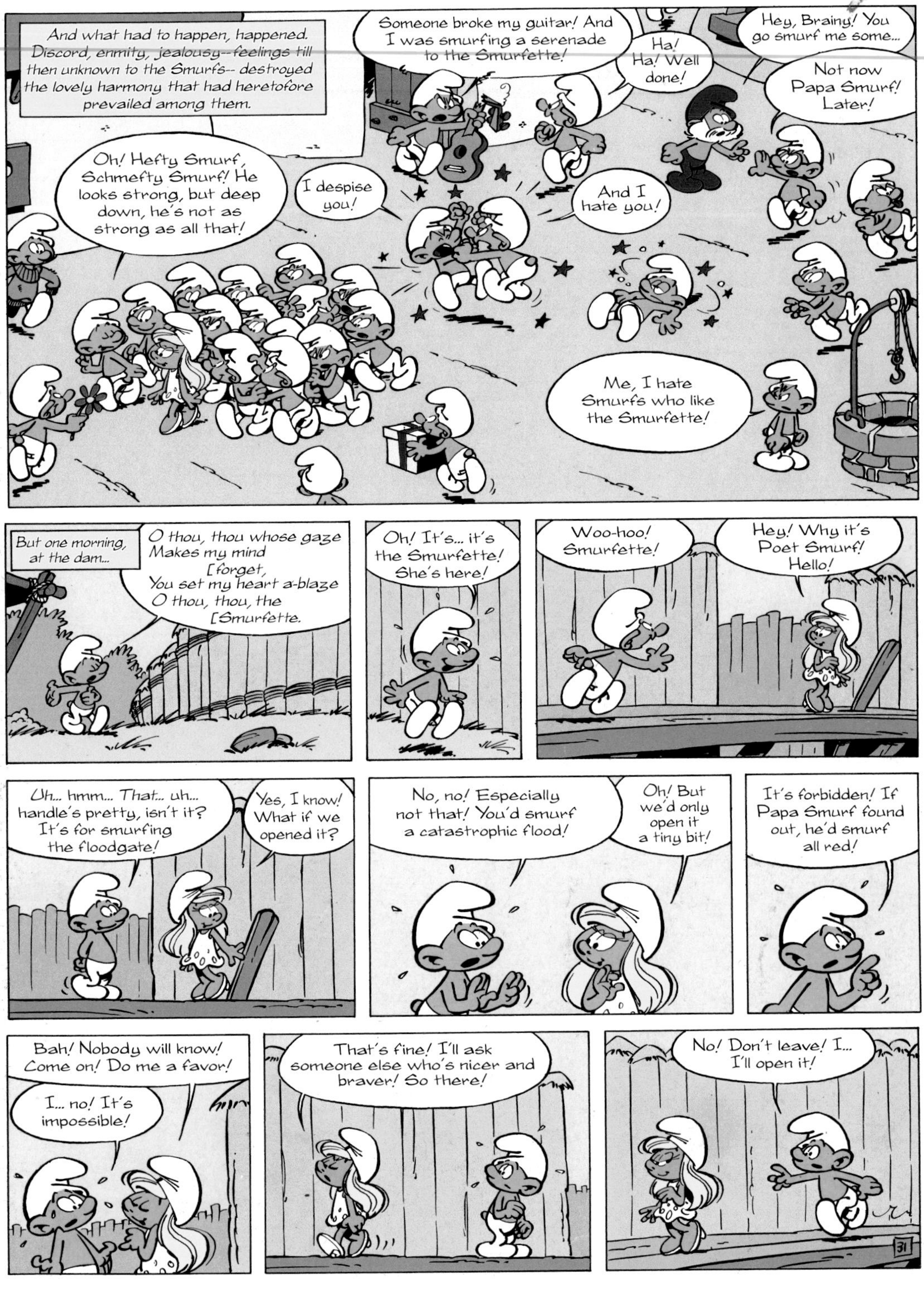

And what had to happen, happened. Discord, enmity, jealousy--feelings till then unknown to the Smurfs-- destroyed the lovely harmony that had heretofore prevailed among them.
Someone broke my guitar! And I was smurfing a serenade to the Smurfette!
Ha! Ha! Well done!
Hey, Brainy! You go smurf me some...
Not now Papa Smurf! Later!
Oh! Hefty Smurf, Schmefty Smurf! He looks strong, but deep down, he's not as strong as all that!
I despise you!
And I hate you!
Me, I hate Smurfs who like the Smurfette!
But one morning, at the dam...
O thou, thou whose gaze Makes my mind [forget, You set my heart a-blaze O thou, thou, the [Smurfette.
Oh! It's... it's the Smurfette! She's here!
Woo-hoo! Smurfette!
Hey! Why it's Poet Smurf! Hello!
Uh... hmm... That... uh... handle's pretty, isn't it? It's for smurfing the floodgate!
Yes, I know! What if we opened it?
No, no! Especially not that! You'd smurf a catastrophic flood!
Oh! But we'd only open it a tiny bit!
It's forbidden! If Papa Smurf found out, he'd smurf all red!
Bah! Nobody will know! Come on! Do me a favor!
I... no! It's impossible!
That's fine! I'll ask someone else who's nicer and braver! So there!
No! Don't leave! I... I'll open it!
31

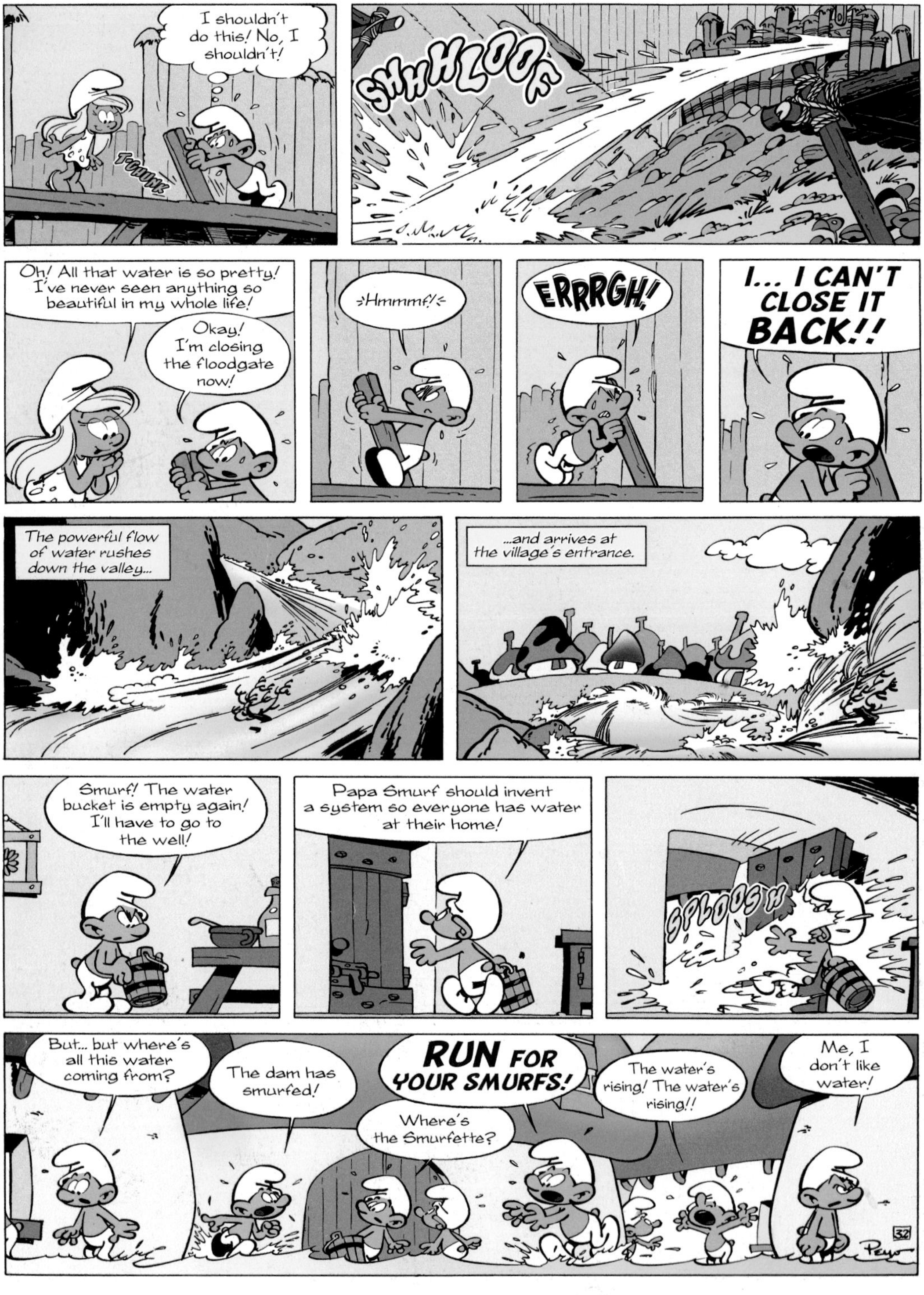
I shouldn't do this! No, I shouldn't!
T-CHUNK
SHHHLOOOF
Oh! All that water is so pretty! I've never seen anything so beautiful in my whole life!
Okay! I'm closing the floodgate now!
Hmmmf!
ERRRGH!
I... I CAN'T CLOSE IT BACK!!
The powerful flow of water rushes down the valley...
...and arrives at the village's entrance.
Smurf! The water bucket is empty again! I'll have to go to the well!
Papa Smurf should invent a system so everyone has water at their home!
SPLOOSH
But... but where's all this water coming from?
The dam has smurfed!
RUN FOR YOUR SMURFS!
Where's the Smurfette?
The water's rising! The water's rising!!
Me, I don't like water!
32
Peyo

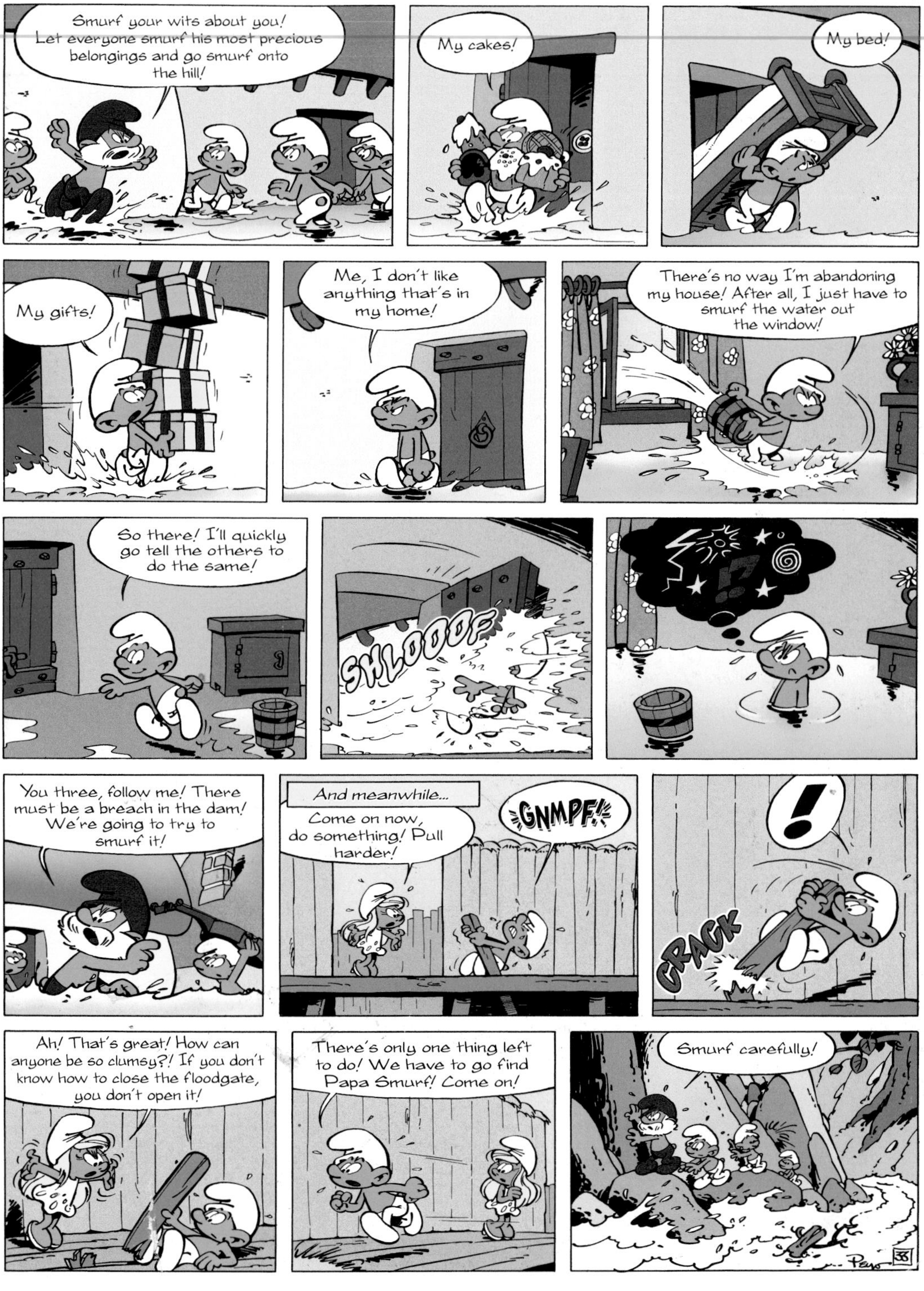

Smurf your wits about you! Let everyone smurf his most precious belongings and go smurf onto the hill!
My cakes!
My bed!
My gifts!
Me, I don't like anything that's in my home!
There's no way I'm abandoning my house! After all, I just have to smurf the water out the window!
So there! I'll quickly go tell the others to do the same!
SHLOOOF
You three, follow me! There must be a breach in the dam! We're going to try to smurf it!
And meanwhile...
Come on now, do something! Pull harder!
GNMPF!
!
CRACK
Ah! That's great! How can anyone be so clumsy?! If you don't know how to close the floodgate, you don't open it!
There's only one thing left to do! We have to go find Papa Smurf! Come on!
Smurf carefully!
Peyo
33

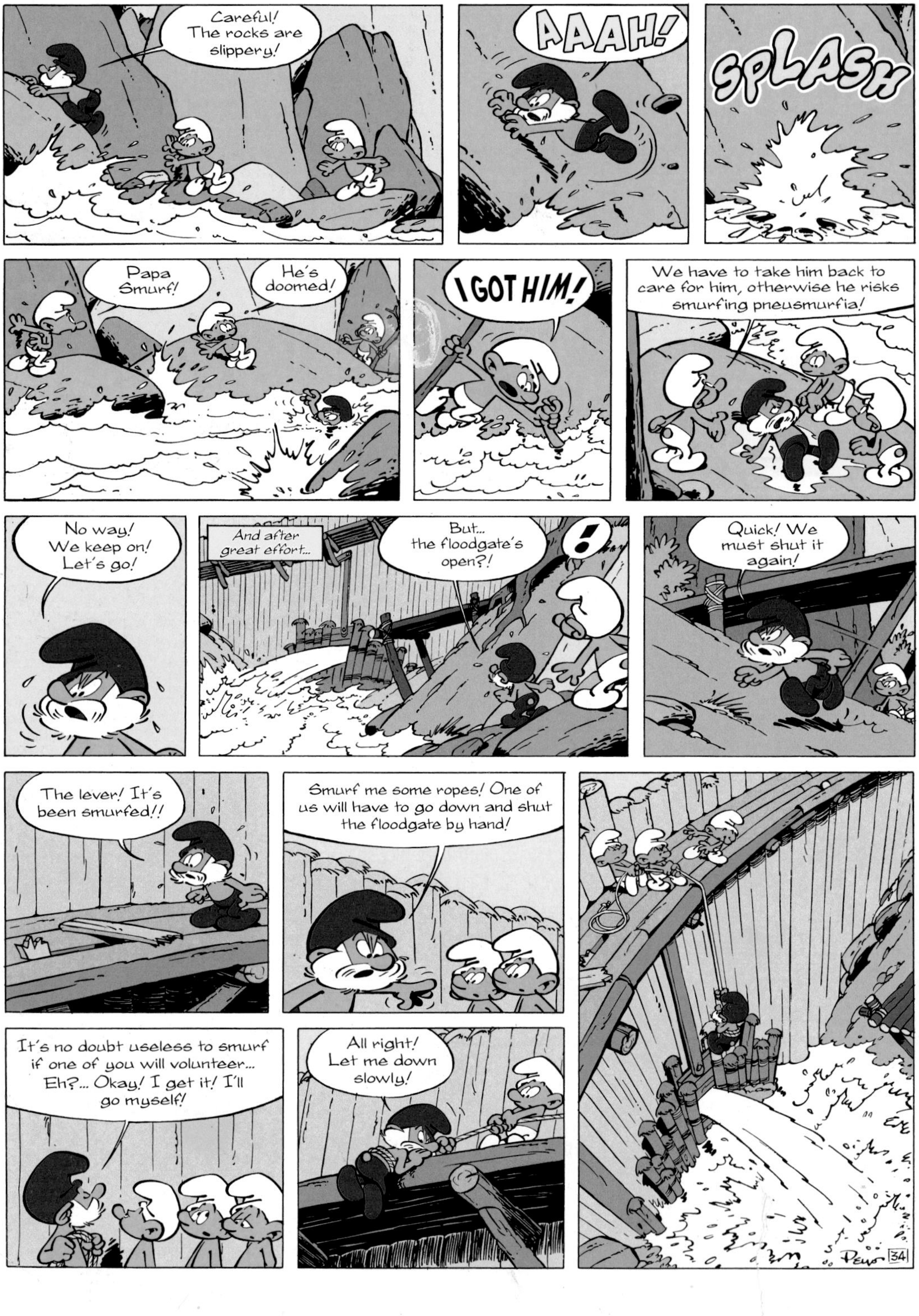
Careful! The rocks are slippery!
AAAH!
SPLASH
Papa Smurf!
He's doomed!
I GOT HIM!
We have to take him back to care for him, otherwise he risks smurfing pneusmurfia!
No way! We keep on! Let's go!
And after great effort...
But... the floodgate's open?!
!
Quick! We must shut it again!
The lever! It's been smurfed!!
Smurf me some ropes! One of us will have to go down and shut the floodgate by hand!
It's no doubt useless to smurf if one of you will volunteer... Eh?... Okay! I get it! I'll go myself!
All right! Let me down slowly!
Peyo
34

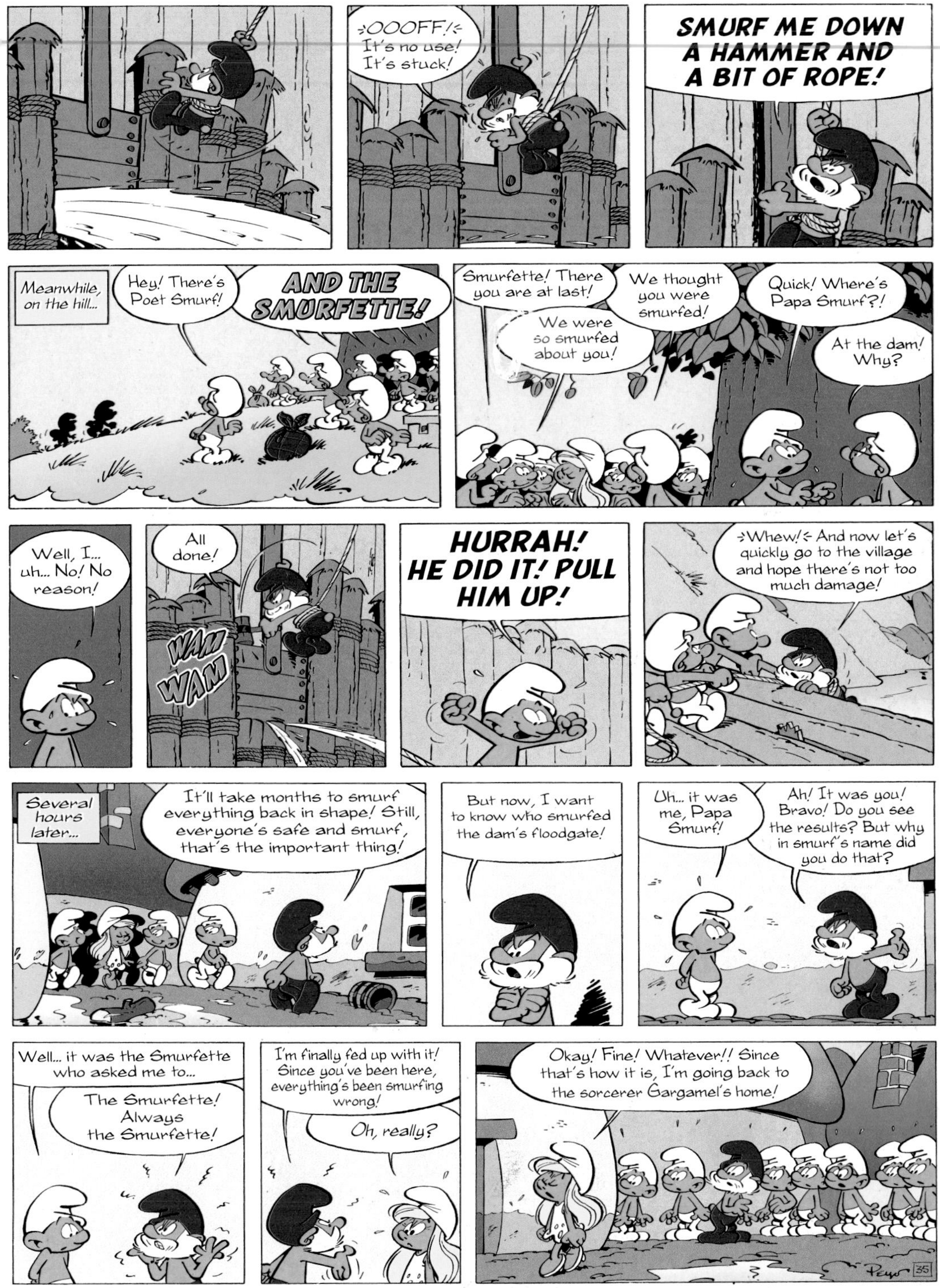

OOOFF! It's no use! It's stuck!
SMURF ME DOWN A HAMMER AND A BIT OF ROPE!
Meanwhile, on the hill...
Hey! There's Poet Smurf!
AND THE SMURFETTE!
Smurfette! There you are at last!
We were so smurfed about you!
We thought you were smurfed!
Quick! Where's Papa Smurf?!
At the dam! Why?
Well, I... uh... No! No reason!
All done!
WAM WAM
HURRAH! HE DID IT! PULL HIM UP!
Whew! And now let's quickly go to the village and hope there's not too much damage!
Several hours later...
It'll take months to smurf everything back in shape! Still, everyone's safe and smurf, that's the important thing!
But now, I want to know who smurfed the dam's floodgate!
Uh... it was me, Papa Smurf!
Ah! It was you! Bravo! Do you see the results? But why in smurf's name did you do that?
Well... it was the Smurfette who asked me to...
The Smurfette! Always the Smurfette!
I'm finally fed up with it! Since you've been here, everything's been smurfing wrong!
Oh, really?
Okay! Fine! Whatever!! Since that's how it is, I'm going back to the sorcerer Gargamel's home!
Peyo 35

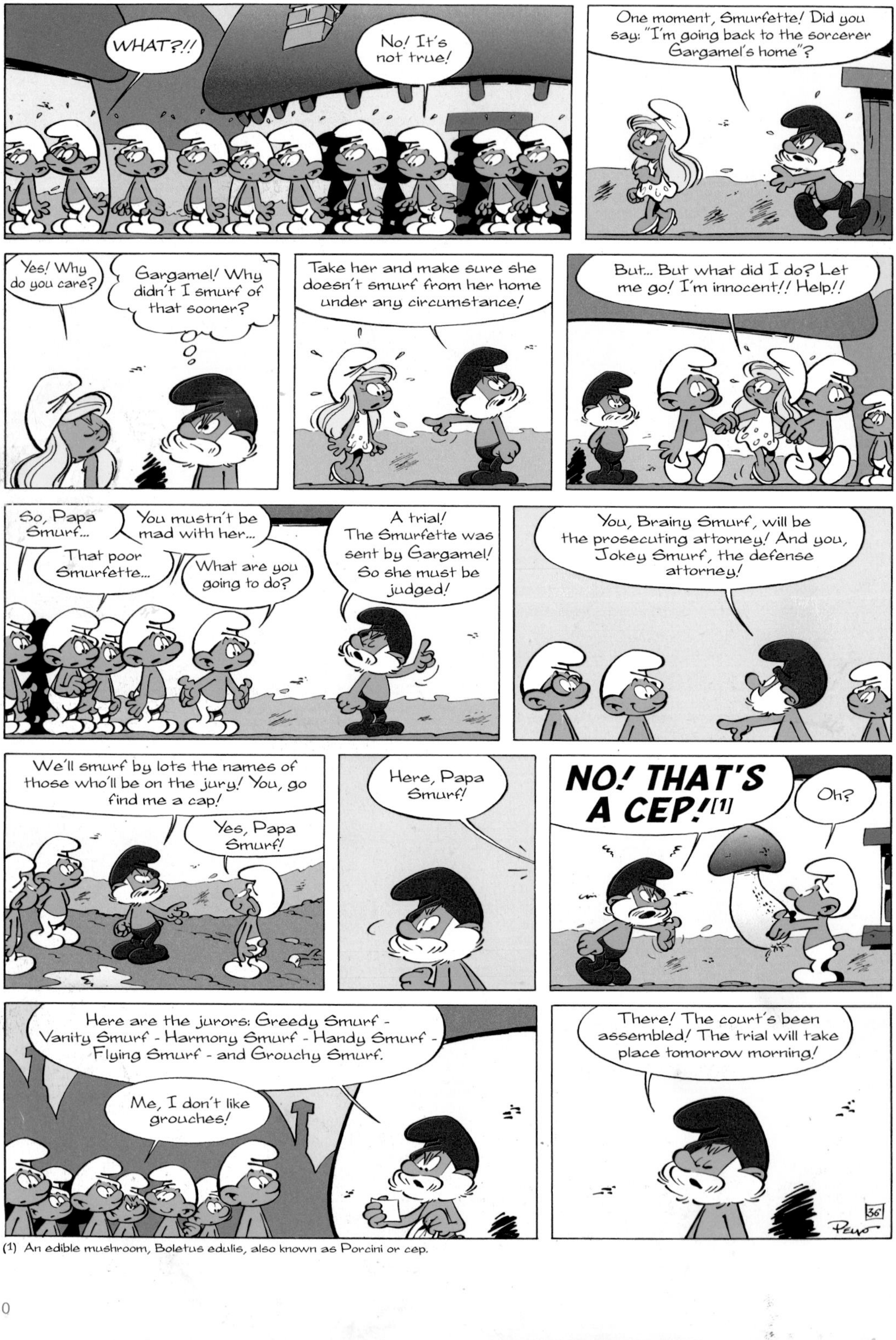
WHAT?!!
No! It's not true!
One moment, Smurfette! Did you say: "I'm going back to the sorcerer Gargamel's home"?
Yes! Why do you care?
Gargamel! Why didn't I smurf of that sooner?
Take her and make sure she doesn't smurf from her home under any circumstance!
But... But what did I do? Let me go! I'm innocent!! Help!!
So, Papa Smurf...
You mustn't be mad with her...
That poor Smurfette...
What are you going to do?
A trial! The Smurfette was sent by Gargamel! So she must be judged!
You, Brainy Smurf, will be the prosecuting attorney! And you, Jokey Smurf, the defense attorney!
We'll smurf by lots the names of those who'll be on the jury! You, go find me a cap!
Yes, Papa Smurf!
Here, Papa Smurf!
NO! THAT'S A CEP![1]
Oh?
Here are the jurors: Greedy Smurf - Vanity Smurf - Harmony Smurf - Handy Smurf - Flying Smurf - and Grouchy Smurf.
Me, I don't like grouches!
There! The court's been assembled! The trial will take place tomorrow morning!
36
Peyo

(1) An edible mushroom, Boletus edulis, also known as Porcini or cep.

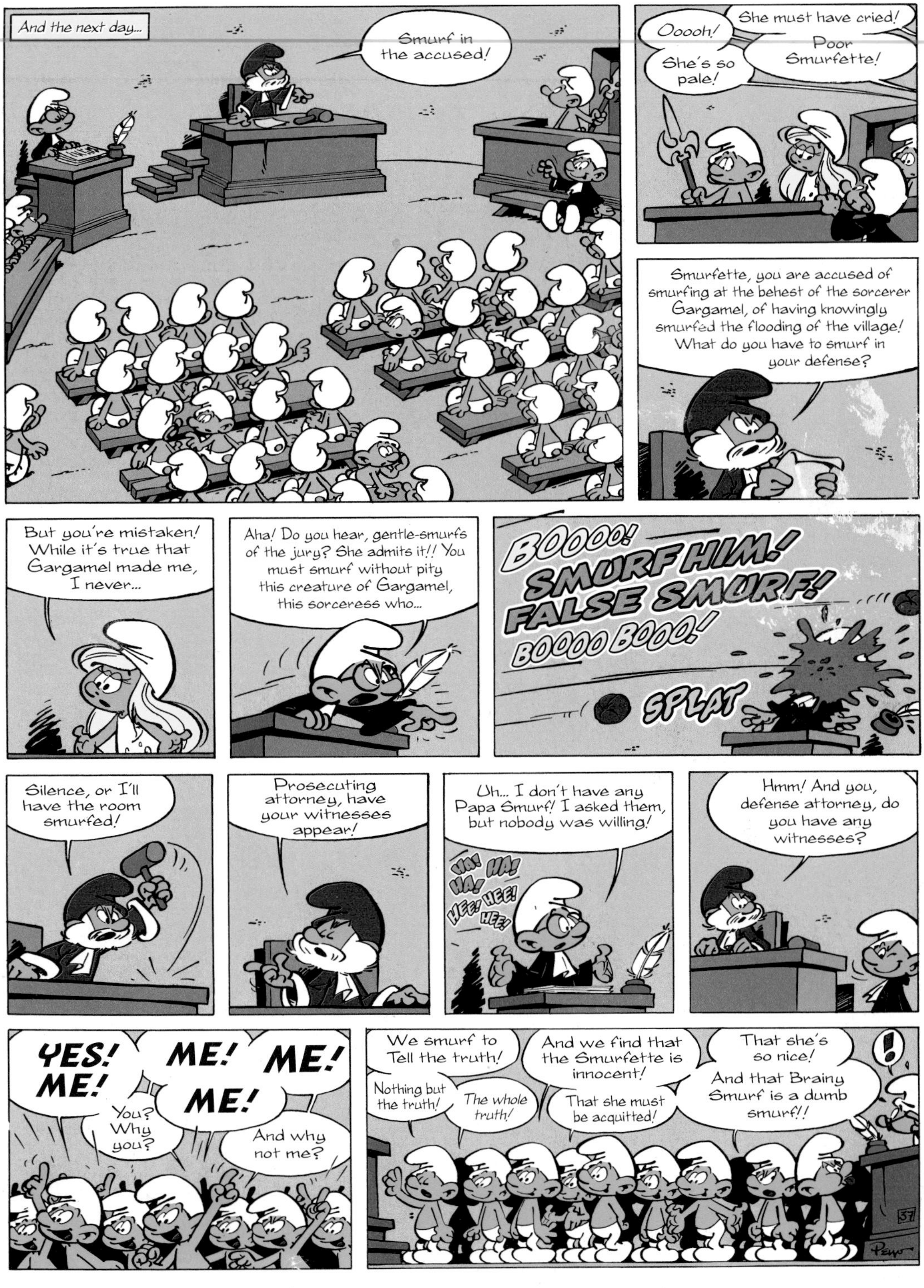
And the next day...
Smurf in the accused!
Ooooh!
She's so pale!
She must have cried!
Poor Smurfette!
Smurfette, you are accused of smurfing at the behest of the sorcerer Gargamel, of having knowingly smurfed the flooding of the village! What do you have to smurf in your defense?
But you're mistaken! While it's true that Gargamel made me, I never...
Aha! Do you hear, gentle-smurfs of the jury? She admits it!! You must smurf without pity this creature of Gargamel, this sorceress who...
BOOOO! SMURF HIM! FALSE SMURF! BOOOO BOOO!
SPLAT
Silence, or I'll have the room smurfed!
Prosecuting attorney, have your witnesses appear!
Uh... I don't have any Papa Smurf! I asked them, but nobody was willing!
HA! HA! HA! HEE! HEE! HEE!
Hmm! And you, defense attorney, do you have any witnesses?
YES! ME!
ME!
ME!
ME!
You? Why you?
And why not me?
We smurf to Tell the truth!
Nothing but the truth!
The whole truth!
And we find that the Smurfette is innocent!
That she must be acquitted!
That she's so nice!
And that Brainy Smurf is a dumb smurf!!
!

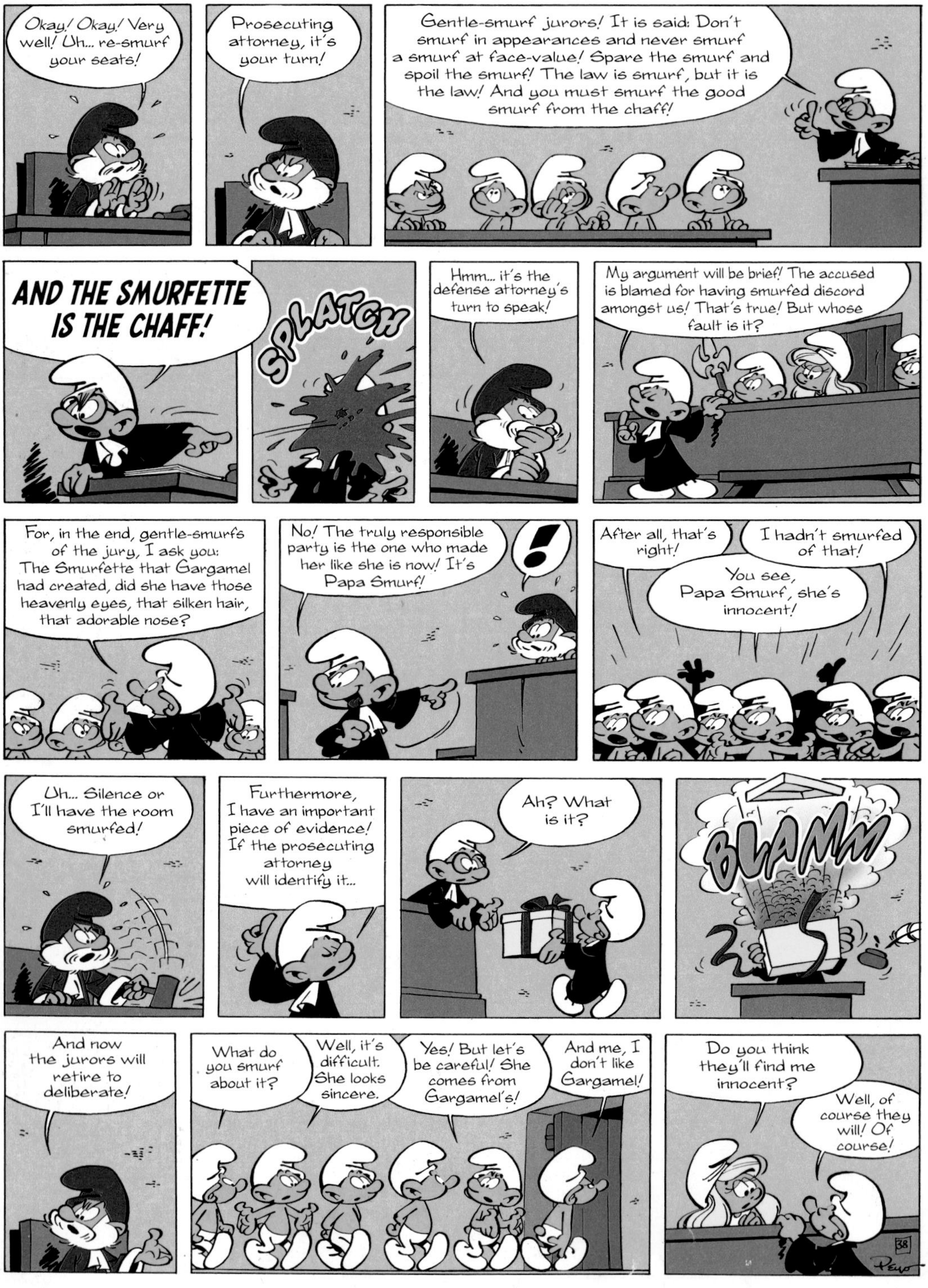
Okay! Okay! Very well! Uh... re-smurf your seats!
Prosecuting attorney, it's your turn!
Gentle-smurf jurors! It is said: Don't smurf in appearances and never smurf a smurf at face-value! Spare the smurf and spoil the smurf! The law is smurf, but it is the law! And you must smurf the good smurf from the chaff!
AND THE SMURFETTE IS THE CHAFF!
SPLATCH
Hmm... it's the defense attorney's turn to speak!
My argument will be brief! The accused is blamed for having smurfed discord amongst us! That's true! But whose fault is it?
For, in the end, gentle-smurfs of the jury, I ask you: The Smurfette that Gargamel had created, did she have those heavenly eyes, that silken hair, that adorable nose?
No! The truly responsible party is the one who made her like she is now! It's Papa Smurf!
!
After all, that's right!
I hadn't smurfed of that!
You see, Papa Smurf, she's innocent!
Uh... Silence or I'll have the room smurfed!
Furthermore, I have an important piece of evidence! If the prosecuting attorney will identify it...
Ah? What is it?
BLAMM
And now the jurors will retire to deliberate!
What do you smurf about it?
Well, it's difficult. She looks sincere.
Yes! But let's be careful! She comes from Gargamel's!
And me, I don't like Gargamel!
Do you think they'll find me innocent?
Well, of course they will! Of course!
38
Peyo

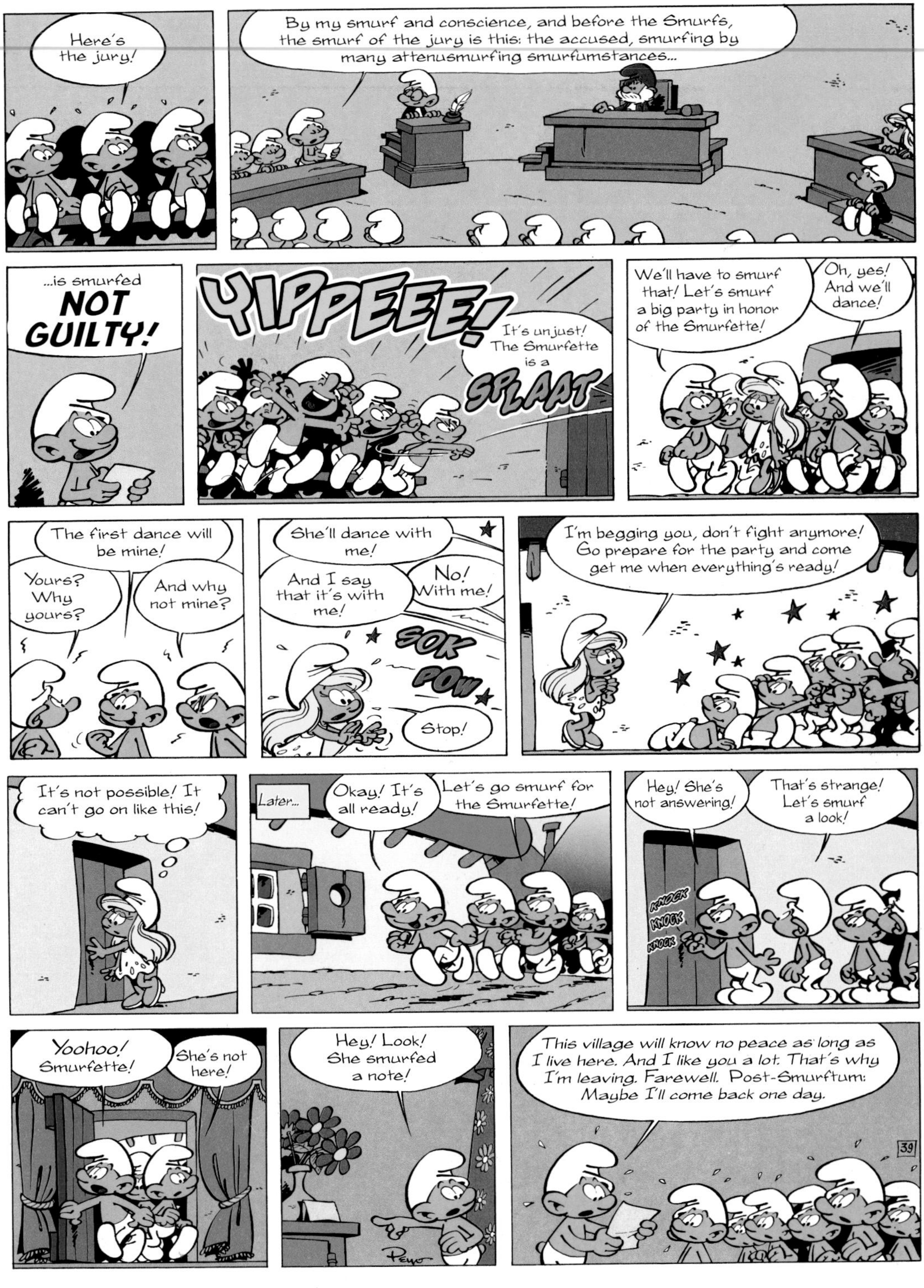

Here's the jury!
By my smurf and conscience, and before the Smurfs, the smurf of the jury is this: the accused, smurfing by many attenusmurfing smurfumstances...
...is smurfed NOT GUILTY!
YIPPEEE!
It's unjust! The Smurfette is a
SPLAAT
We'll have to smurf that! Let's smurf a big party in honor of the Smurfette!
Oh, yes! And we'll dance!
The first dance will be mine!
Yours? Why yours?
And why not mine?
She'll dance with me!
And I say that it's with me!
No! With me!
SOK
POW
Stop!
I'm begging you, don't fight anymore! Go prepare for the party and come get me when everything's ready!
It's not possible! It can't go on like this!
Later...
Okay! It's all ready!
Let's go smurf for the Smurfette!
Hey! She's not answering!
That's strange! Let's smurf a look!
KNOCK
KNOCK
KNOCK
Yoohoo! Smurfette!
She's not here!
Hey! Look! She smurfed a note!
Peyo
This village will know no peace as long as I live here. And I like you a lot. That's why I'm leaving. Farewell. Post-Smurftum: Maybe I'll come back one day.
39

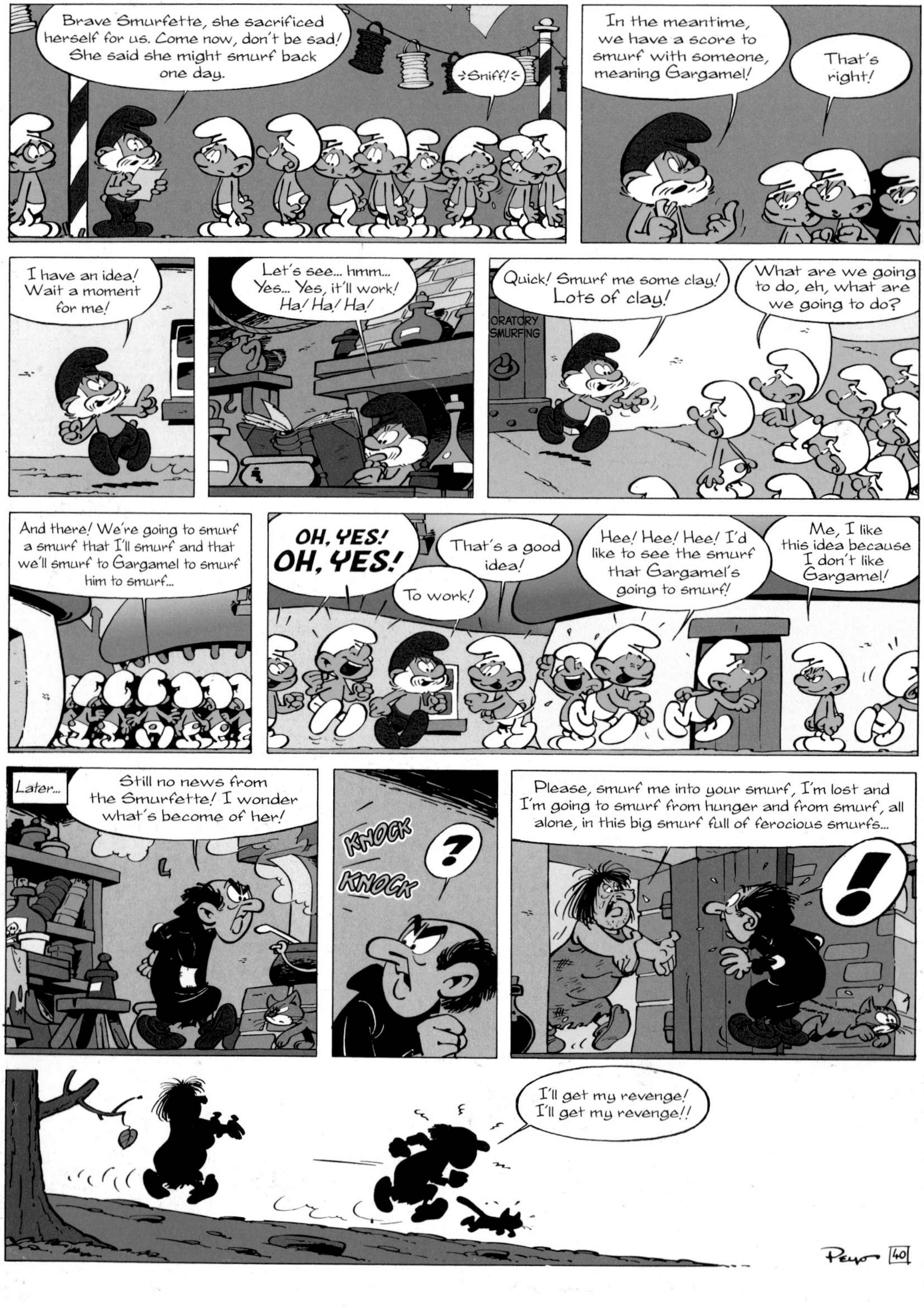
Brave Smurfette, she sacrificed herself for us. Come now, don't be sad! She said she might smurf back one day.
Sniff!
In the meantime, we have a score to smurf with someone, meaning Gargamel!
That's right!
I have an idea! Wait a moment for me!
Let's see... hmm... Yes... Yes, it'll work! Ha! Ha! Ha!
ORATORY SMURFING
Quick! Smurf me some clay! Lots of clay!
What are we going to do, eh, what are we going to do?
And there! We're going to smurf a smurf that I'll smurf and that we'll smurf to Gargamel to smurf him to smurf...
OH, YES! OH, YES!
To work!
That's a good idea!
Hee! Hee! Hee! I'd like to see the smurf that Gargamel's going to smurf!
Me, I like this idea because I don't like Gargamel!
Later...
Still no news from the Smurfette! I wonder what's become of her!
KNOCK KNOCK
?
Please, smurf me into your smurf, I'm lost and I'm going to smurf from hunger and from smurf, all alone, in this big smurf full of ferocious smurfs...
!
I'll get my revenge! I'll get my revenge!!
Peyo
40

THE HUNGRY SMURFS

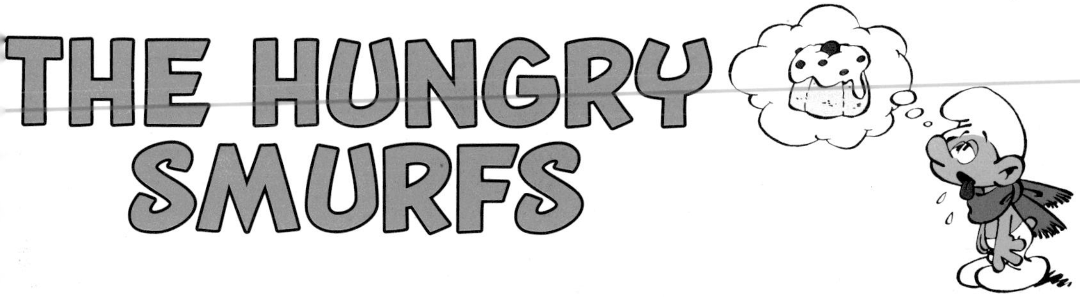

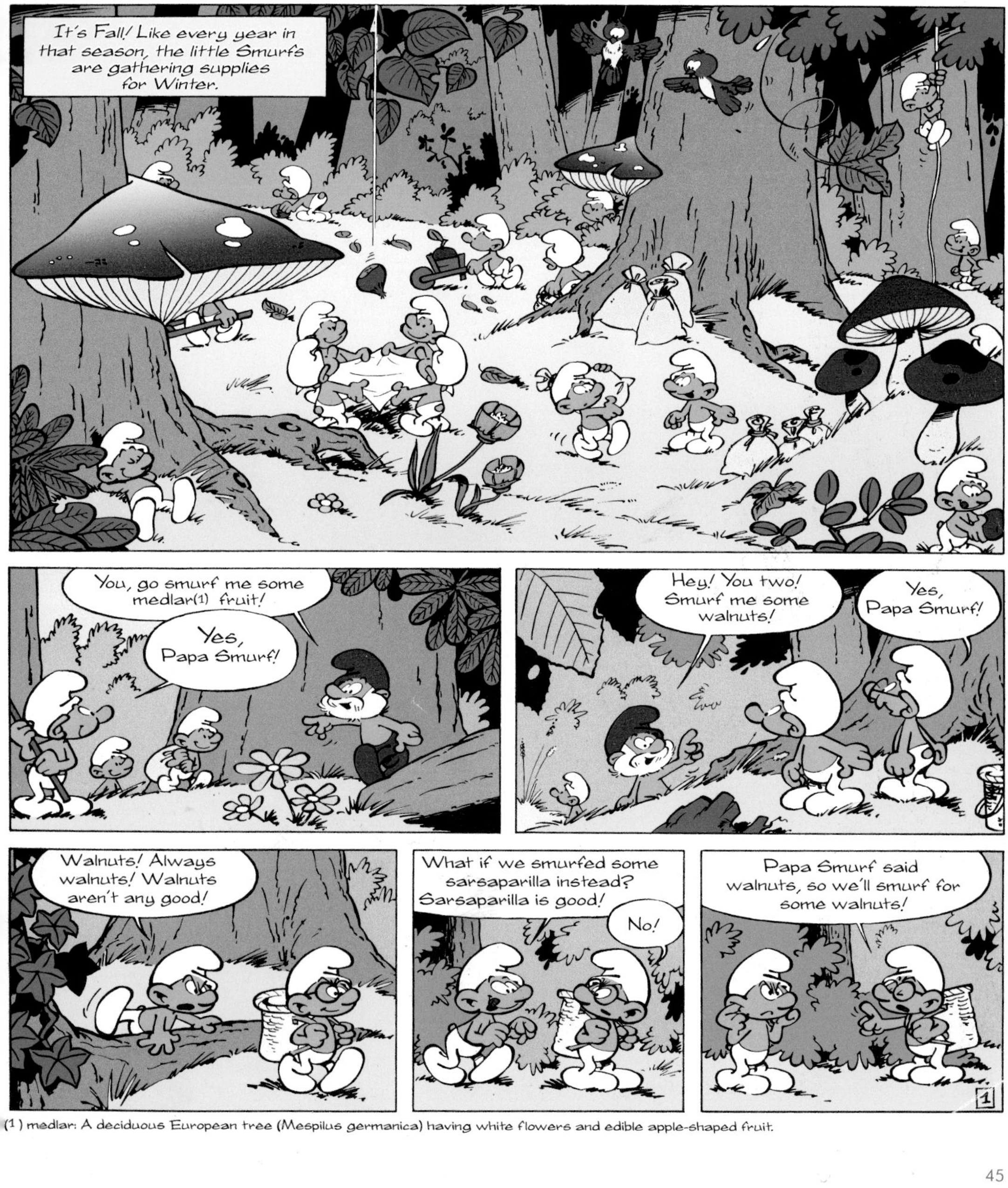

It's Fall! Like every year in that season, the little Smurfs are gathering supplies for Winter.
You, go smurf me some medlar(1) fruit!
Yes, Papa Smurf!
Hey! You two! Smurf me some walnuts!
Yes, Papa Smurf!
1
Walnuts! Always walnuts! Walnuts aren't any good!
What if we smurfed some sarsaparilla instead? Sarsaparilla is good!
No!
Papa Smurf said walnuts, so we'll smurf for some walnuts!
1

(1) medlar: A deciduous European tree (Mespilus germanica) having white flowers and edible apple-shaped fruit.

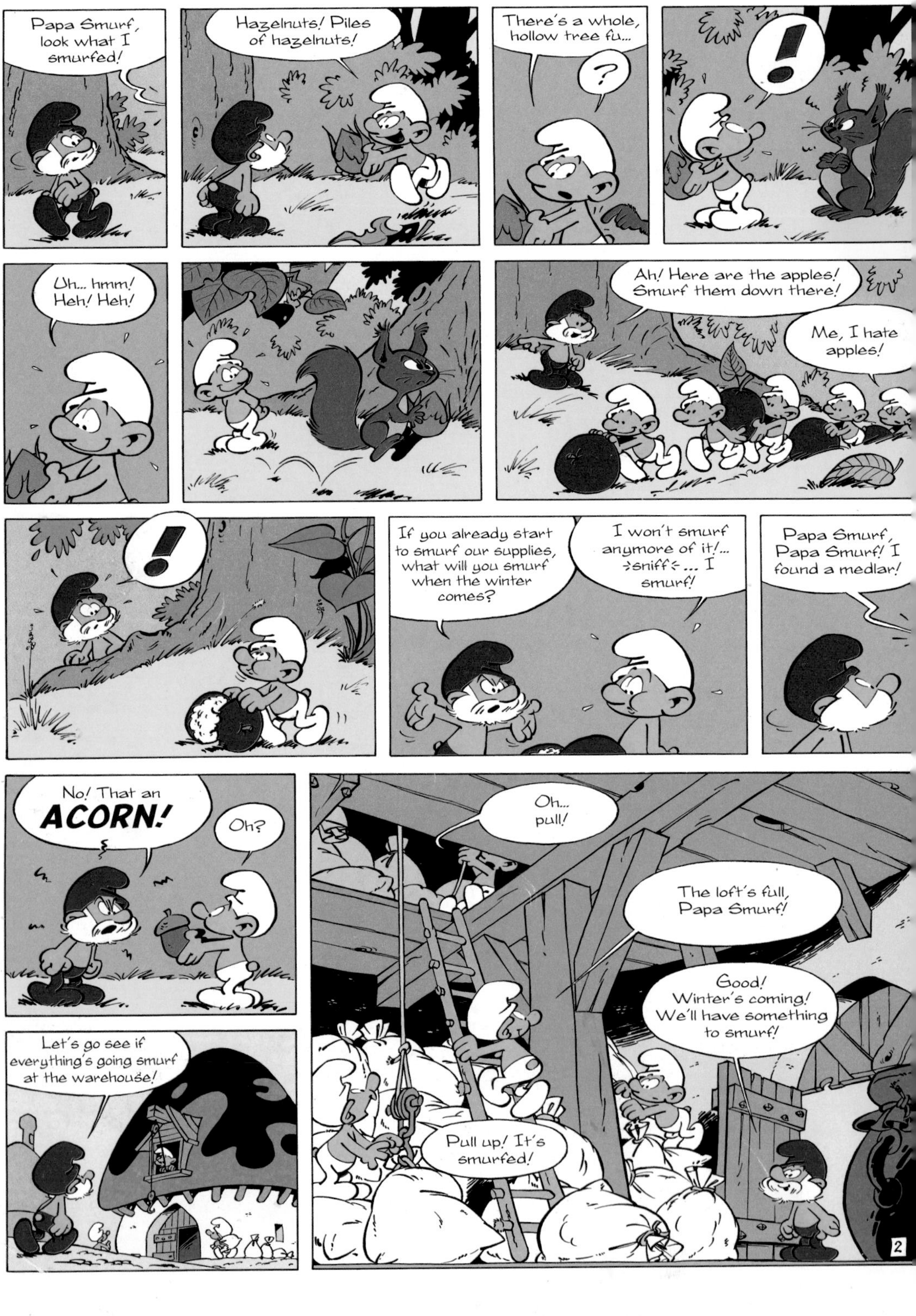

Papa Smurf, look what I smurfed!
Hazelnuts! Piles of hazelnuts!
There's a whole, hollow tree fu...
?
!
Uh... hmm! Heh! Heh!
Ah! Here are the apples! Smurf them down there!
Me, I hate apples!
!
If you already start to smurf our supplies, what will you smurf when the winter comes?
I won't smurf anymore of it!... ⋗sniff⋖... I smurf!
Papa Smurf, Papa Smurf! I found a medlar!
No! That an ACORN!
Oh?
Oh... pull!
The loft's full, Papa Smurf!
Good! Winter's coming! We'll have something to smurf!
Let's go see if everything's going smurf at the warehouse!
Pull up! It's smurfed!
2

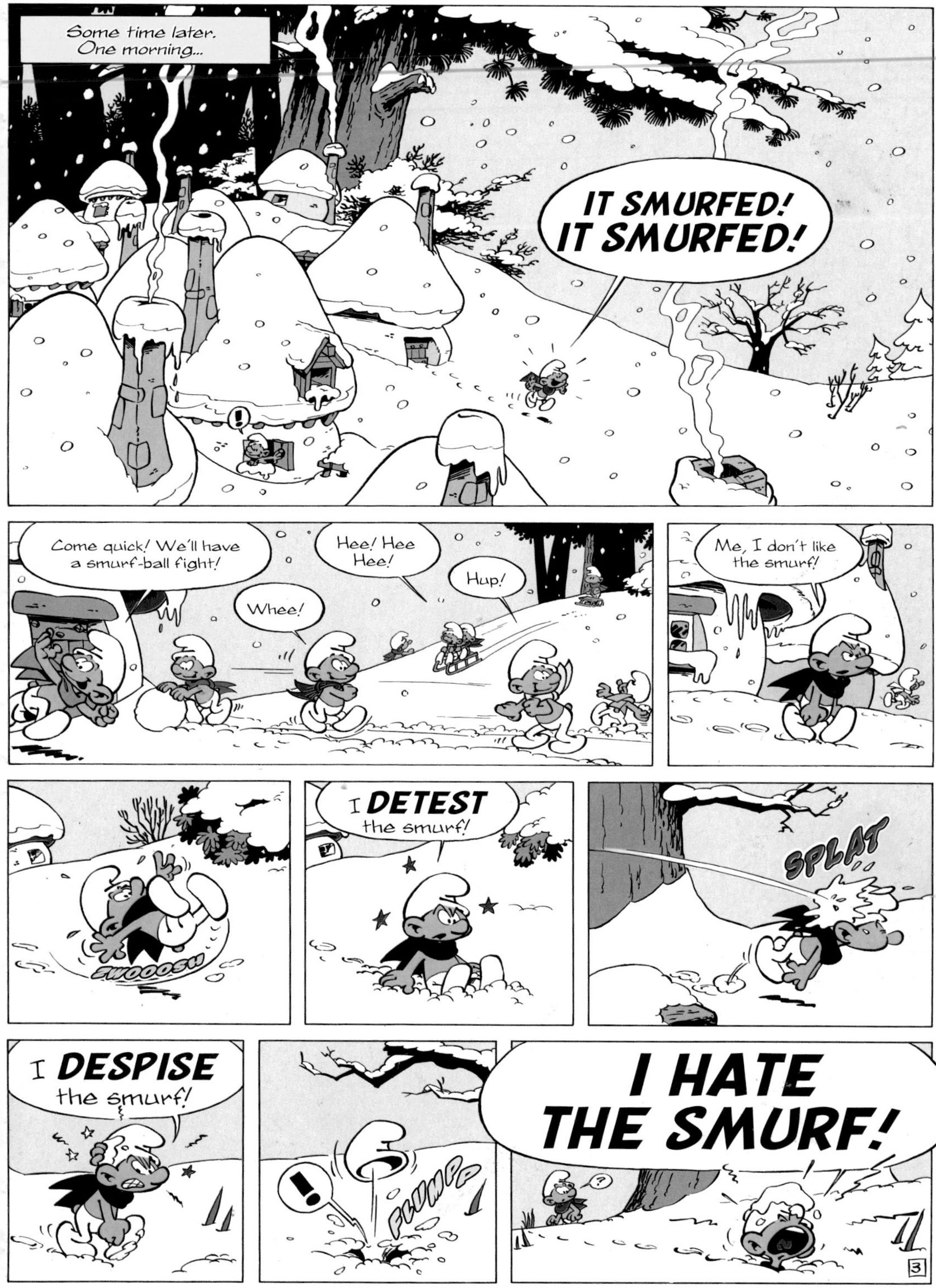

Some time later. One morning...
IT SMURFED! IT SMURFED!
Come quick! We'll have a smurf-ball fight!
Whee!
Hee! Hee Hee!
Hup!
Me, I don't like the smurf!
ZWOOOSH
I DETEST the smurf!
SPLAT
I DESPISE the smurf!
FLUMPP
I HATE THE SMURF!
3

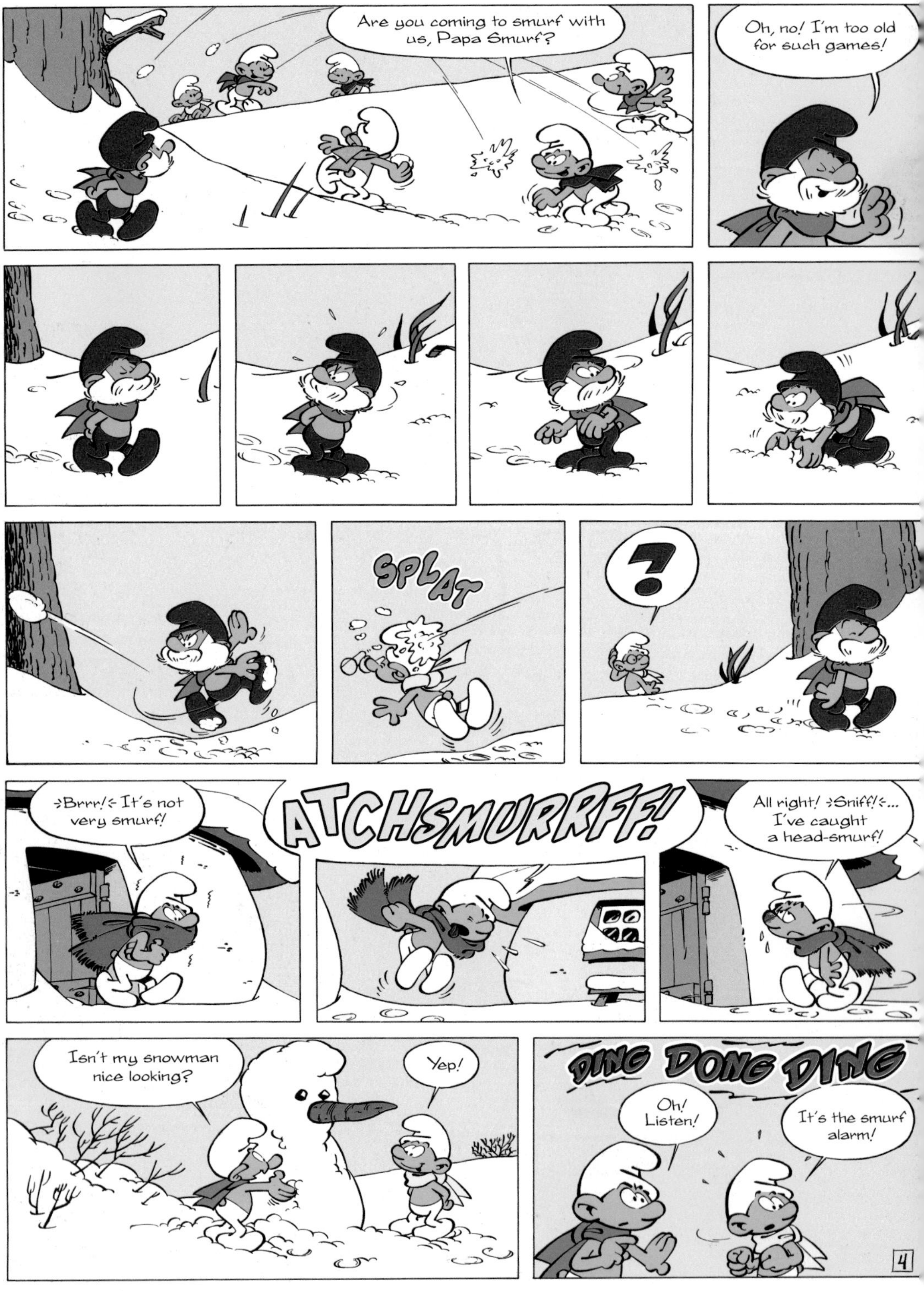
Are you coming to smurf with us, Papa Smurf?
Oh, no! I'm too old for such games!
SPLAT
?
Brrr! It's not very smurf!
ATCHSMURRFF!
All right! Sniff! ... I've caught a head-smurf!
Isn't my snowman nice looking?
Yep!
DING DONG DING
Oh! Listen!
It's the smurf alarm!
4

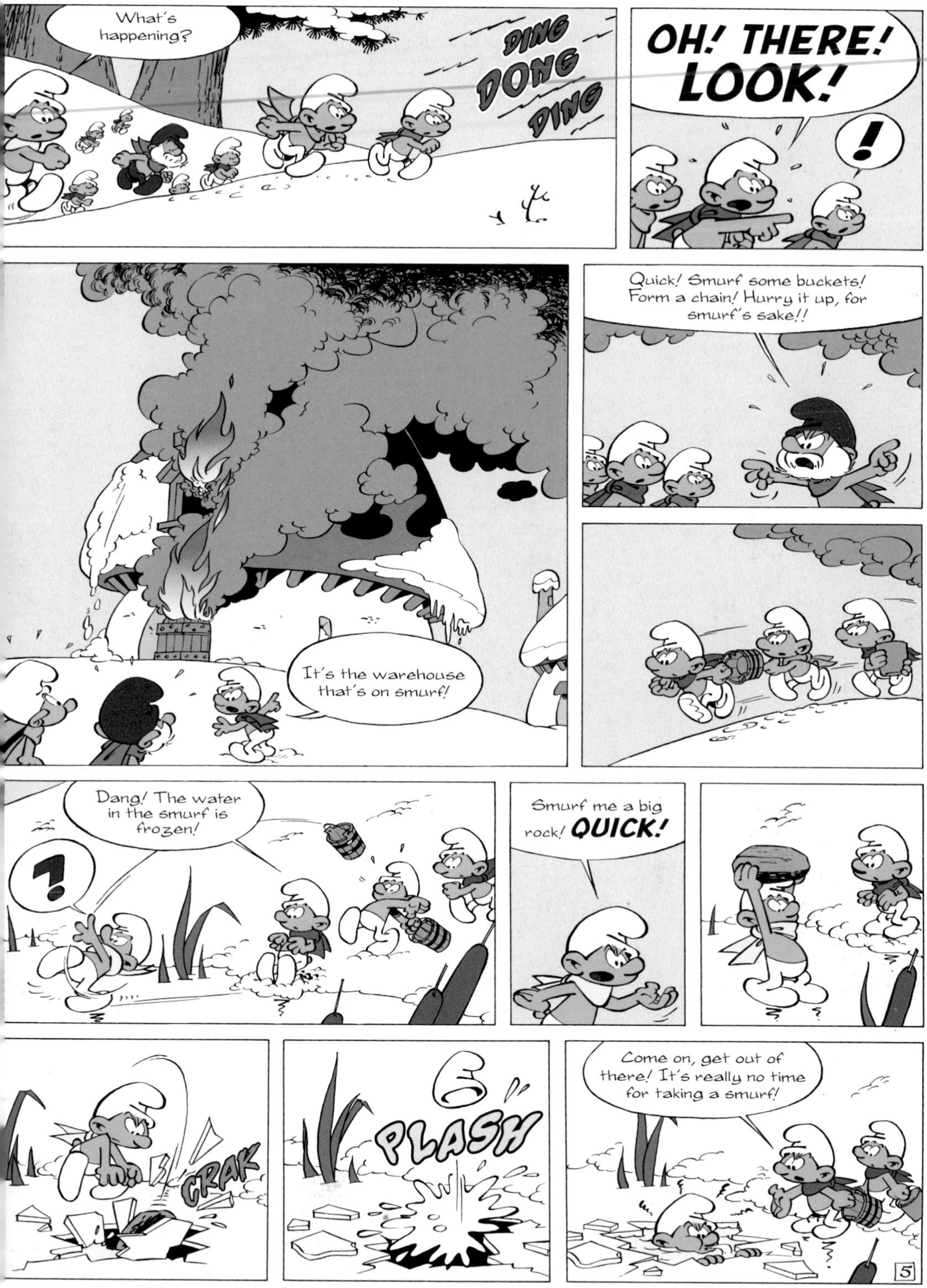

What's happening?
DING DONG DING
OH! THERE! LOOK!
!
It's the warehouse that's on smurf!
Quick! Smurf some buckets! Form a chain! Hurry it up, for smurf's sake!!
Dang! The water in the smurf is frozen!
?
Smurf me a big rock! QUICK!
CRAK
PLASH
Come on, get out of there! It's really no time for taking a smurf!
5

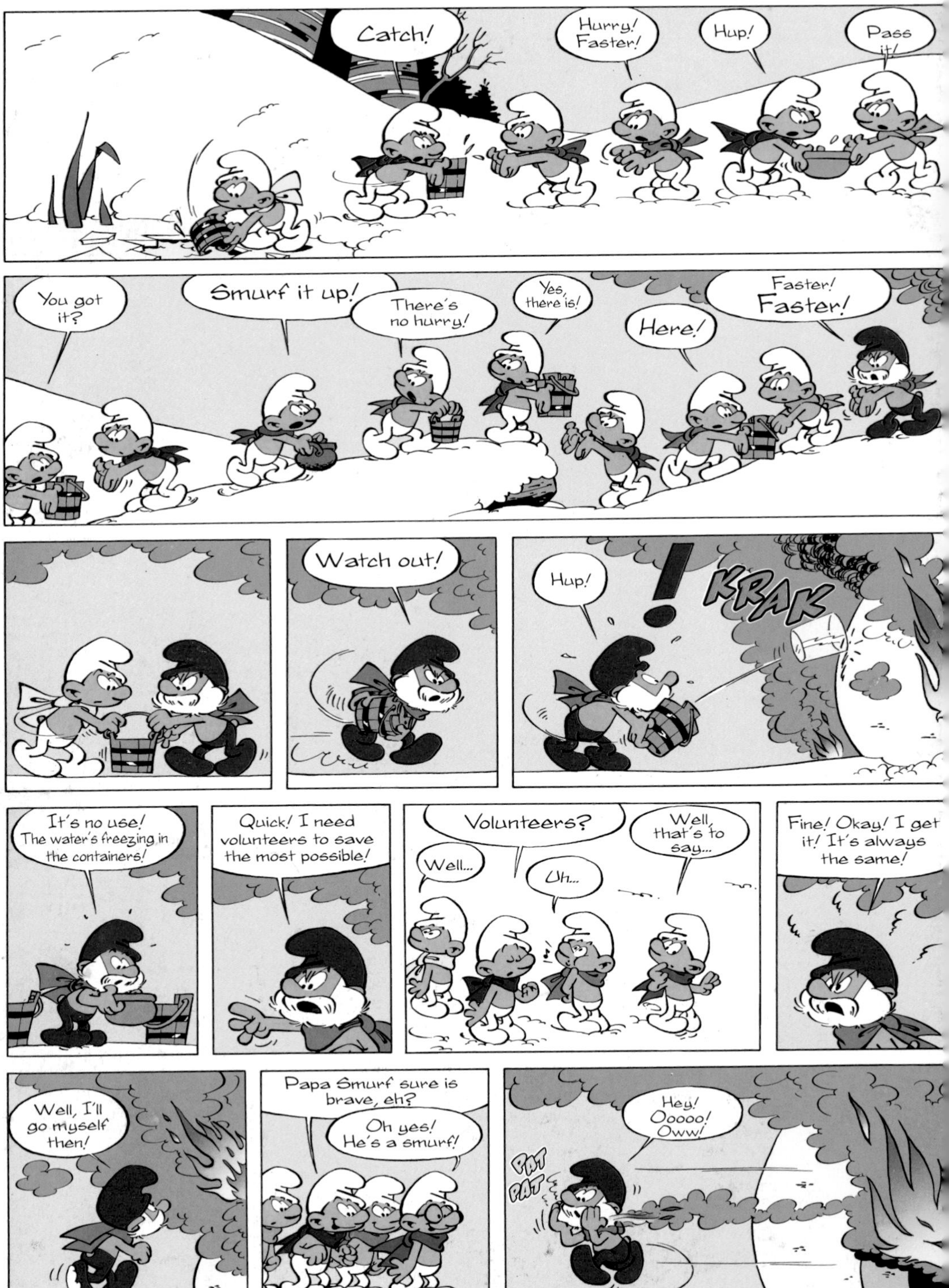
Catch!
Hurry! Faster!
Hup!
Pass it!
You got it?
Smurf it up!
There's no hurry!
Yes, there is!
Here!
Faster! Faster!
Watch out!
Hup!
!
KRAK
It's no use! The water's freezing in the containers!
Quick! I need volunteers to save the most possible!
Volunteers?
Well...
Uh...
Well, that's to say...
Fine! Okay! I get it! It's always the same!
Well, I'll go myself then!
Papa Smurf sure is brave, eh?
Oh yes! He's a smurf!
Hey! Ooooo! Oww!
PAT PAT
6

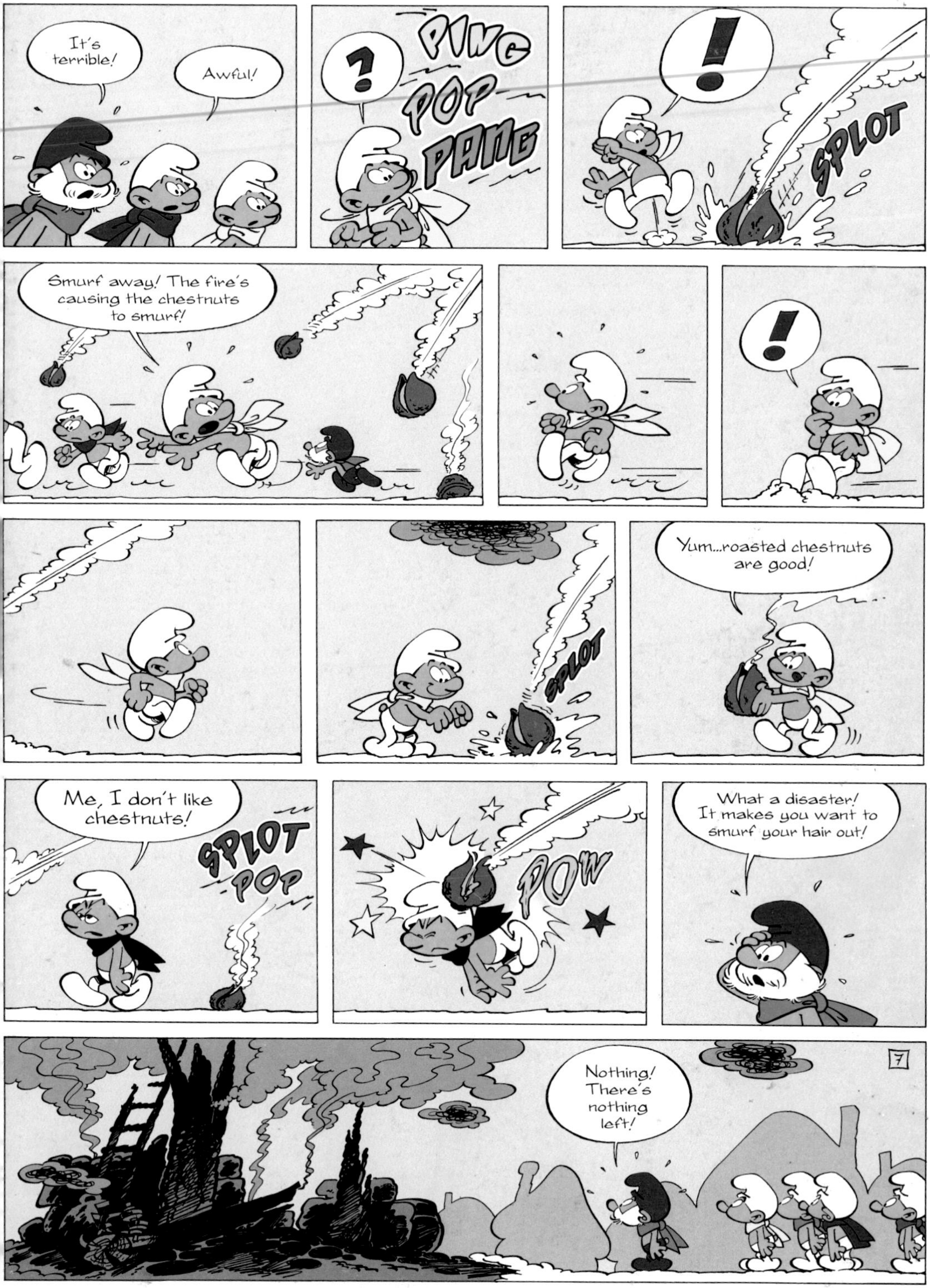
It's terrible!
Awful!
?
PING
POP
PANG
!
SPLOT
Smurf away! The fire's causing the chestnuts to smurf!
!
SPLOT
Yum...roasted chestnuts are good!
Me, I don't like chestnuts!
SPLOT
POP
POW
What a disaster! It makes you want to smurf your hair out!
7
Nothing! There's nothing left!

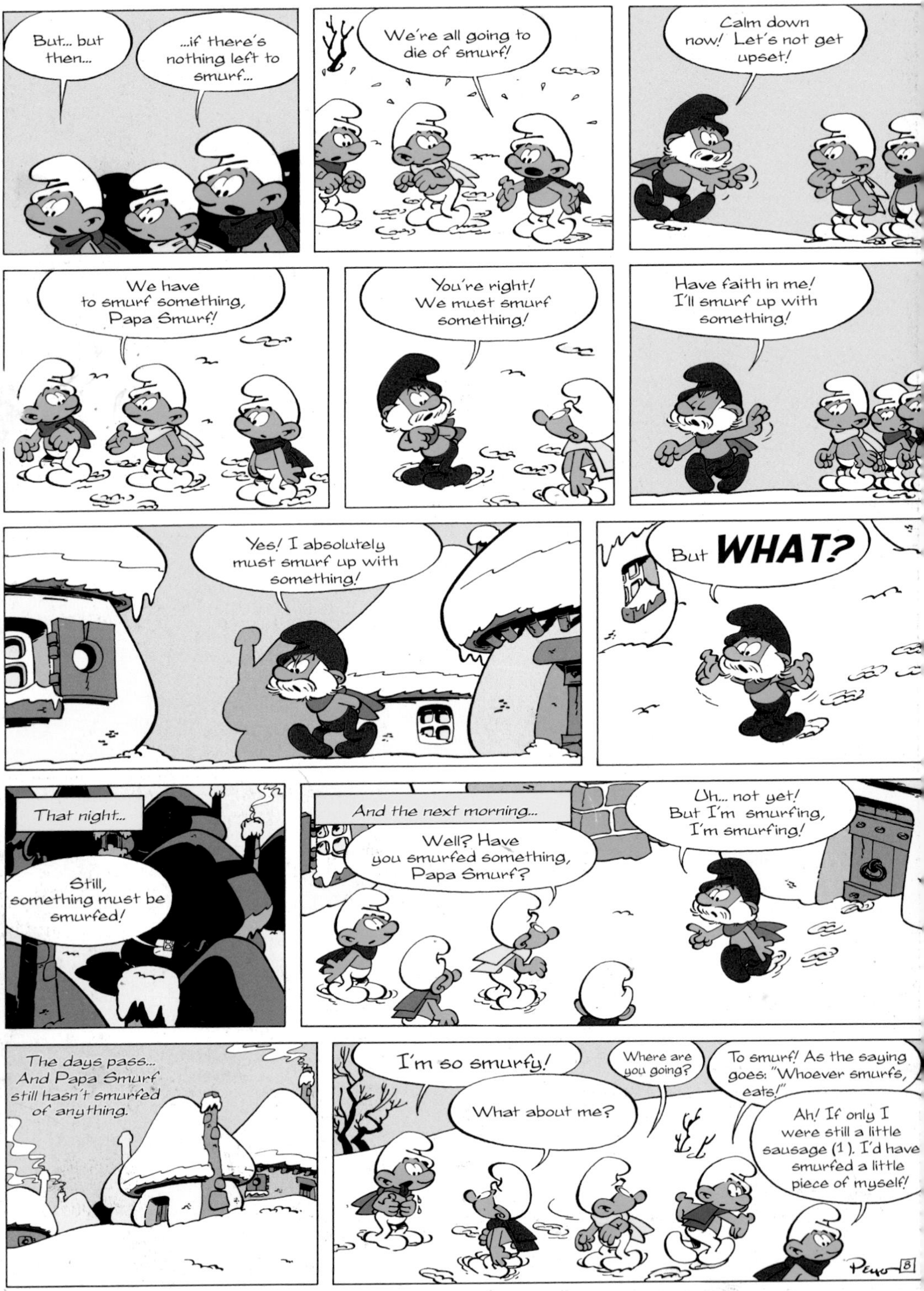

But... but then...
...if there's nothing left to smurf...
We're all going to die of smurf!
Calm down now! Let's not get upset!
We have to smurf something, Papa Smurf!
You're right! We must smurf something!
Have faith in me! I'll smurf up with something!
Yes! I absolutely must smurf up with something!
But WHAT?
That night...
Still, something must be smurfed!
And the next morning...
Well? Have you smurfed something, Papa Smurf?
Uh... not yet! But I'm smurfing, I'm smurfing!
The days pass... And Papa Smurf still hasn't smurfed of anything.
I'm so smurfy!
What about me?
Where are you going?
To smurf! As the saying goes: "Whoever smurfs, eats!"
Ah! If only I were still a little sausage (1). I'd have smurfed a little piece of myself!
Peyo
8

(1) See SMURFS Graphic Novel #5 "The Smurfs and the Egg."

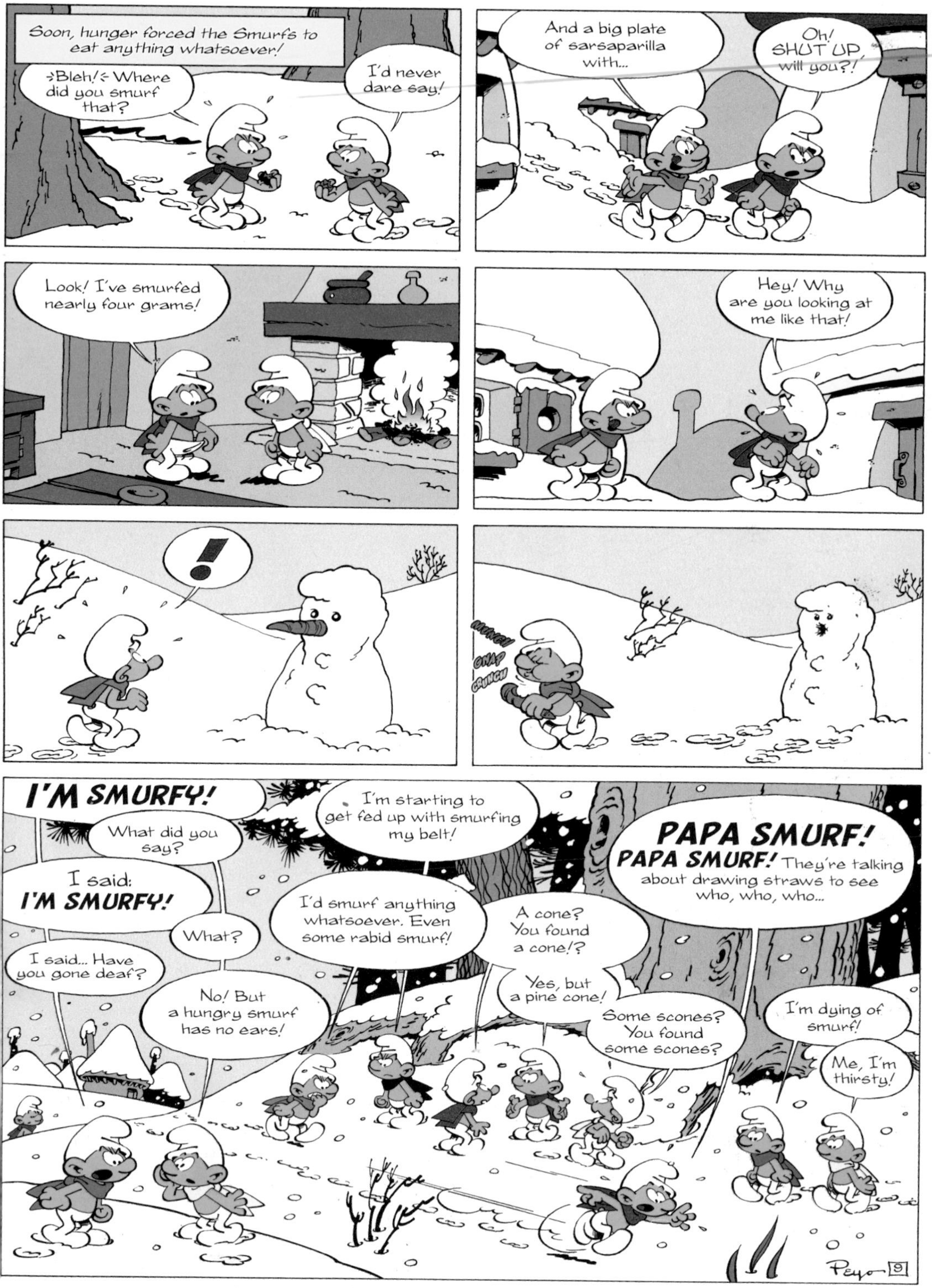
Soon, hunger forced the Smurfs to eat anything whatsoever!
›Bleh!‹ Where did you smurf that?
I'd never dare say!
And a big plate of sarsaparilla with...
Oh! SHUT UP, will you?!
Look! I've smurfed nearly four grams!
Hey! Why are you looking at me like that!
!
I'M SMURFY!
What did you say?
I said: I'M SMURFY!
What?
I said... Have you gone deaf?
No! But a hungry smurf has no ears!
I'm starting to get fed up with smurfing my belt!
I'd smurf anything whatsoever. Even some rabid smurf!
A cone? You found a cone!?
Yes, but a pine cone!
Some scones? You found some scones?
PAPA SMURF! PAPA SMURF! They're talking about drawing straws to see who, who, who...
I'm dying of smurf!
Me, I'm thirsty!
Peyo 9

HEY! SMURF! COME QUICK!

?

I FOUND SOMETHING TO SMURF!!

Can it be true?

No, not really! Ha! Ha! Ha! I got you, eh?

Jokey Smurf!

⸓Pff!⸓ He has no sense of humor!

SCRATCH SCRATCH SCRATCH

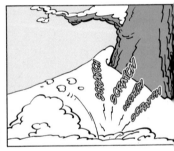

SCRATCH SCRATCH SCRATCH SCRATCH

There's nothing left, Papa Smurf! Not even the tiniest root!

This can't go on!

There's only one thing left for us to do!

Smurfs! Faced with the famine that's threatening us, I've decided we must abandon the Smurf Village!

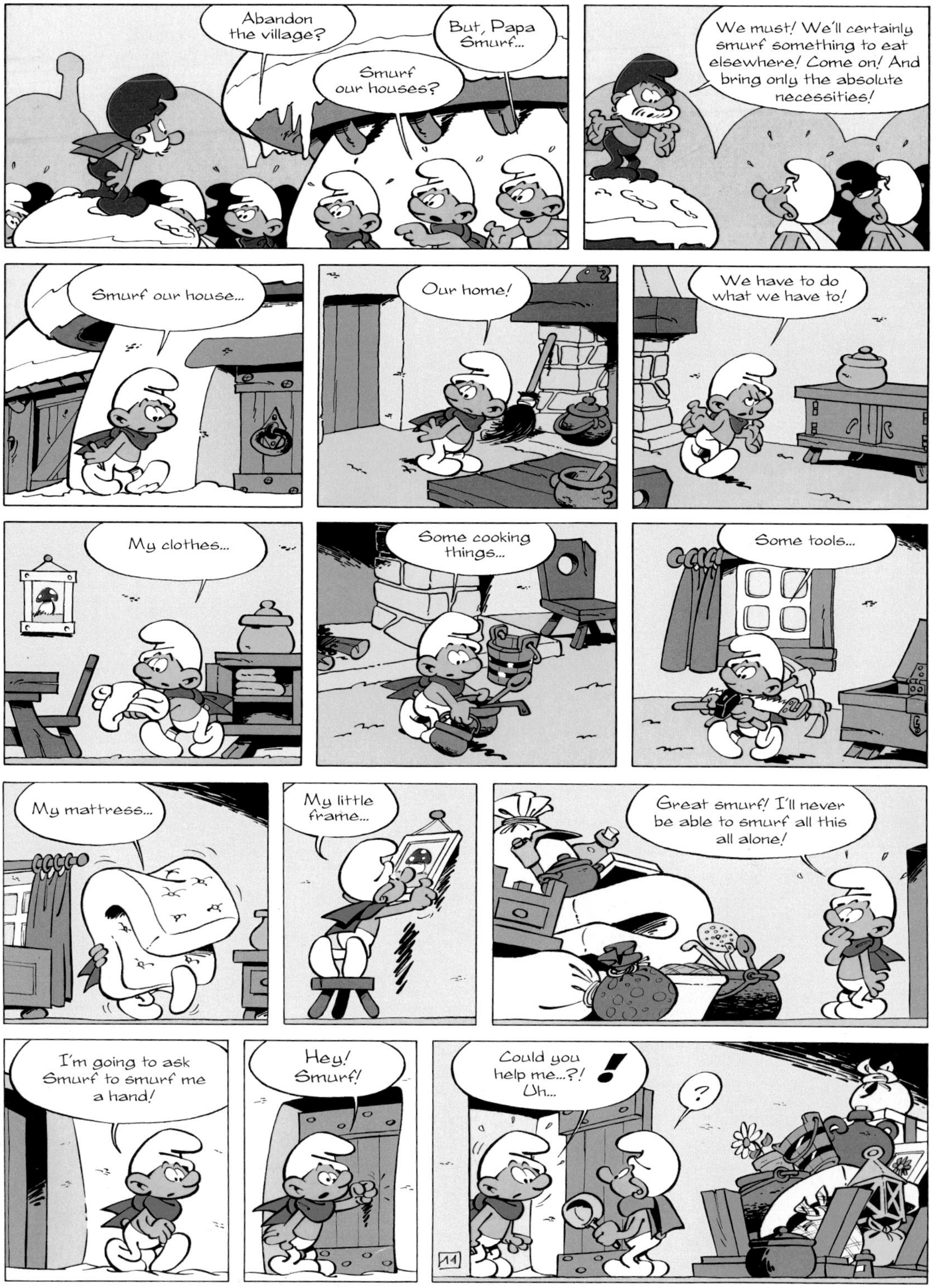
Abandon the village?
Smurf our houses?
But, Papa Smurf...
We must! We'll certainly smurf something to eat elsewhere! Come on! And bring only the absolute necessities!
Smurf our house...
Our home!
We have to do what we have to!
My clothes...
Some cooking things...
Some tools...
My mattress...
My little frame...
Great smurf! I'll never be able to smurf all this all alone!
I'm going to ask Smurf to smurf me a hand!
Hey! Smurf!
Could you help me...?! Uh...
?
!

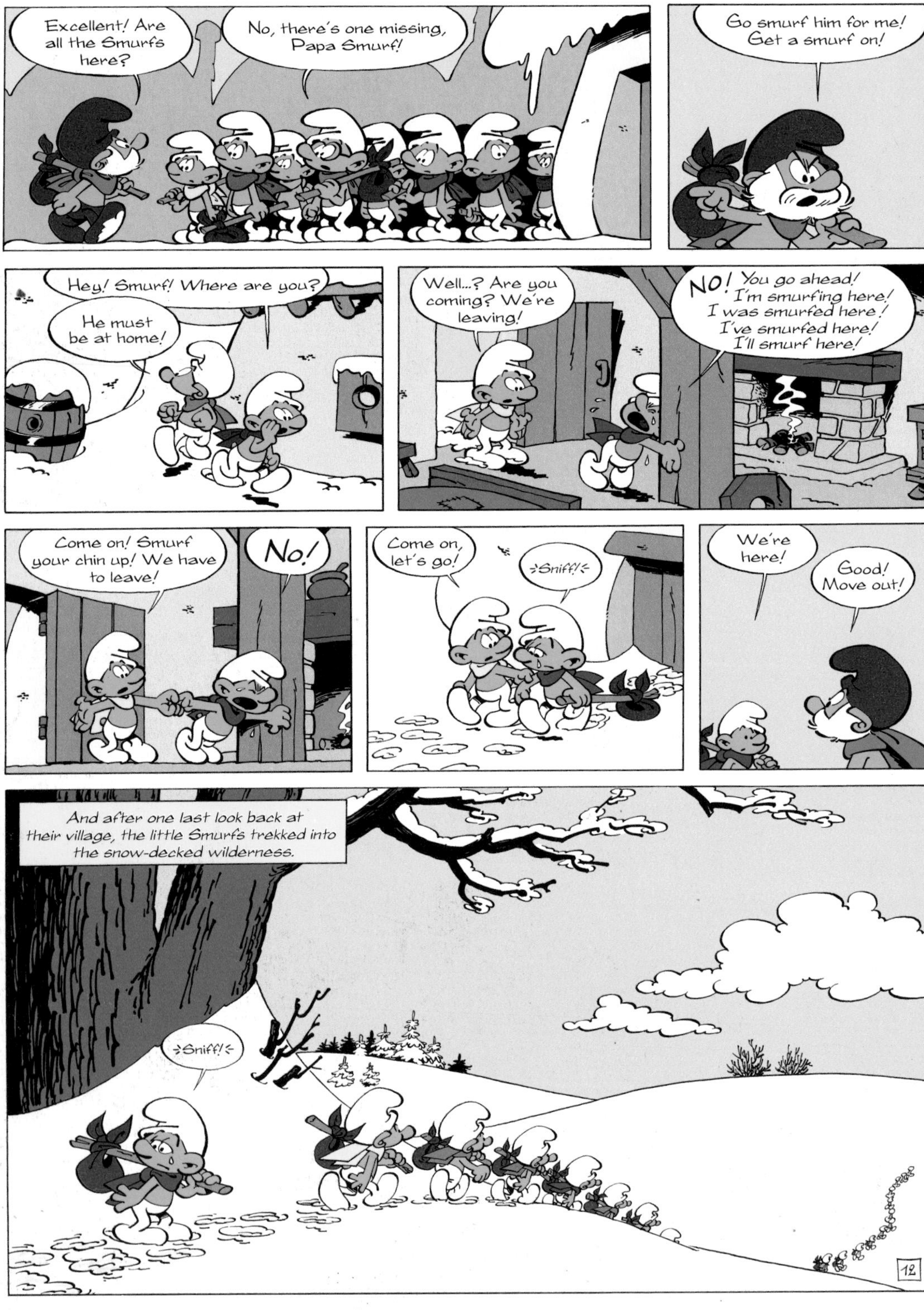

Excellent! Are all the Smurfs here?
No, there's one missing, Papa Smurf!
Go smurf him for me! Get a smurf on!
Hey! Smurf! Where are you?
He must be at home!
Well...? Are you coming? We're leaving!
NO! You go ahead! I'm smurfing here! I was smurfed here! I've smurfed here! I'll smurf here!
Come on! Smurf your chin up! We have to leave!
No!
Come on, let's go!
Sniff!
We're here!
Good! Move out!
And after one last look back at their village, the little Smurfs trekked into the snow-decked wilderness.
Sniff!
12

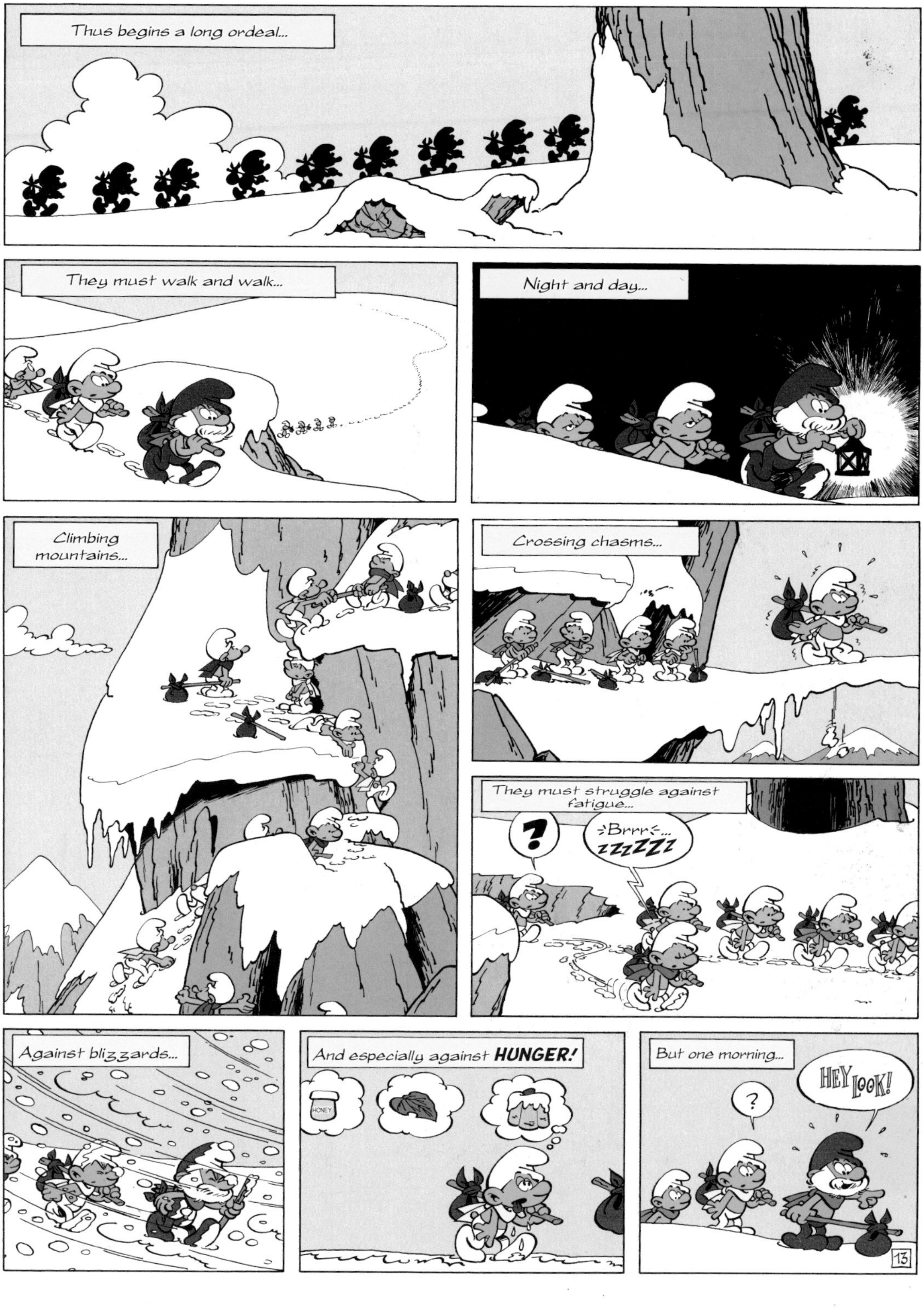
Thus begins a long ordeal...
They must walk and walk...
Night and day...
Climbing mountains...
Crossing chasms...
They must struggle against fatigue...
?
Brrr...
ZZZZZZ
Against blizzards...
And especially against HUNGER!
HONEY
But one morning...
?
HEY LOOK!
13

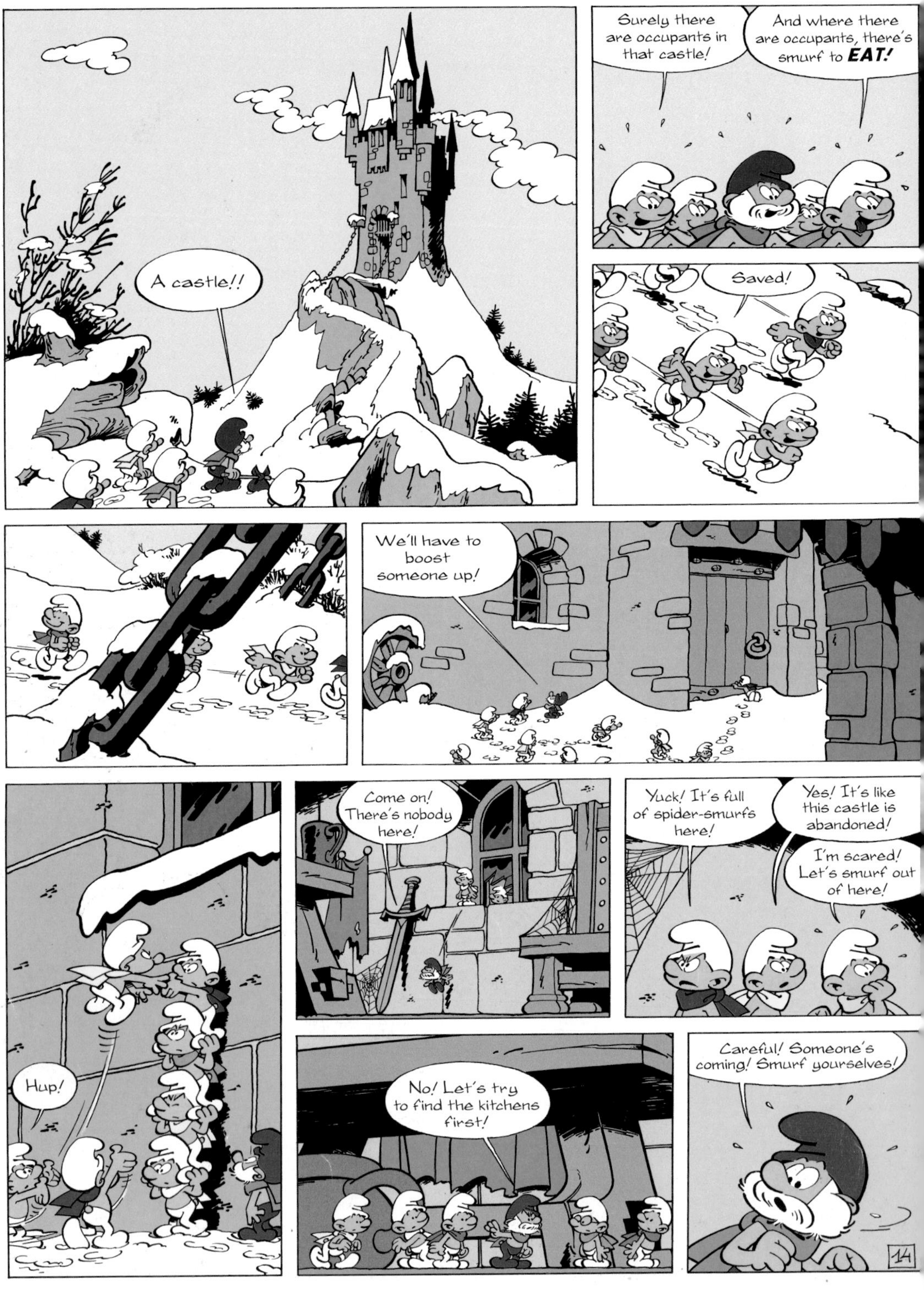
A castle!!
Surely there are occupants in that castle!
And where there are occupants, there's smurf to EAT!
Saved!
We'll have to boost someone up!
Hup!
Come on! There's nobody here!
Yuck! It's full of spider-smurfs here!
Yes! It's like this castle is abandoned!
I'm scared! Let's smurf out of here!
No! Let's try to find the kitchens first!
Careful! Someone's coming! Smurf yourselves!
14

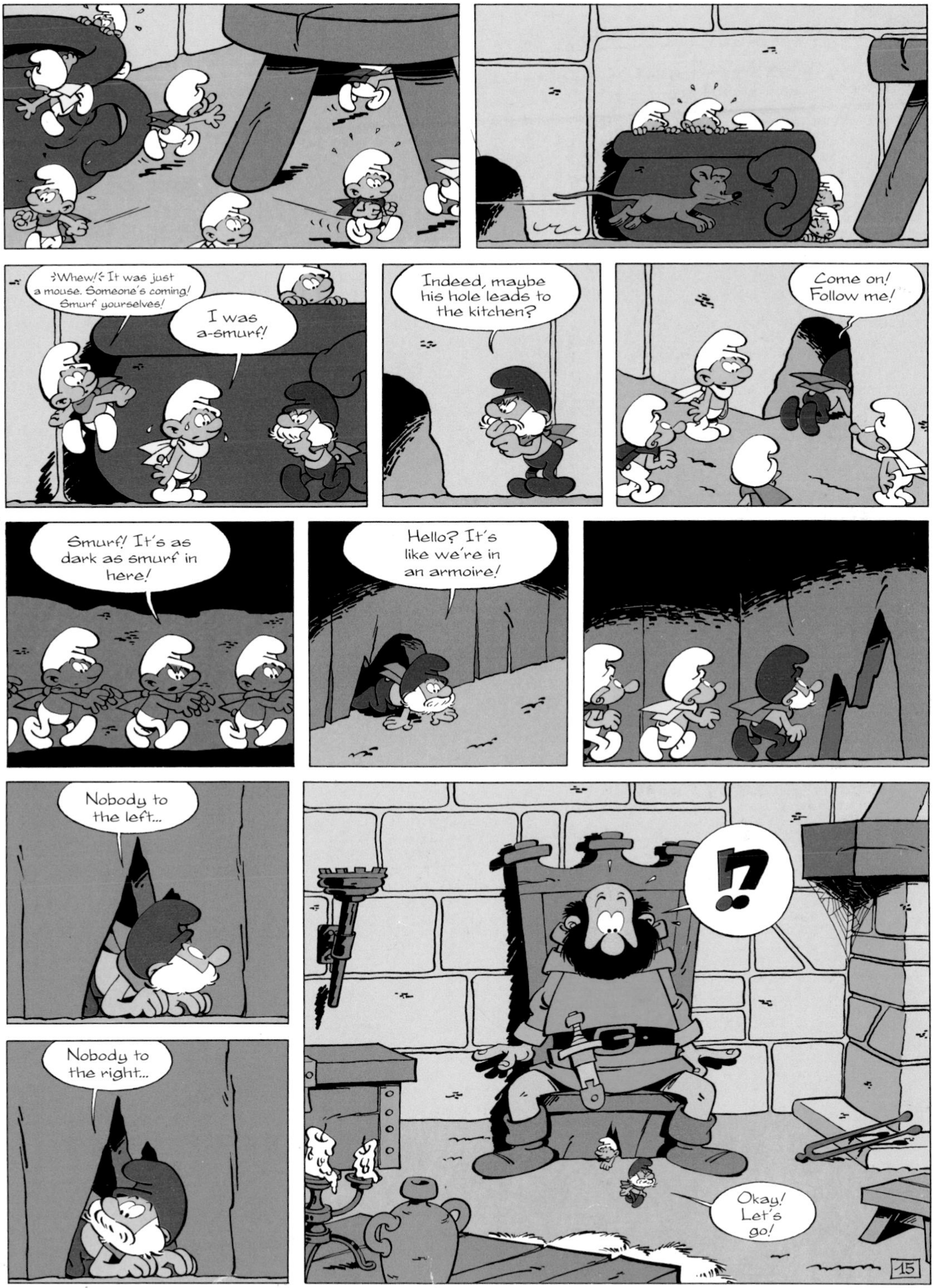

Whew! It was just a mouse. Someone's coming! Smurf yourselves!
I was a-smurf!
Indeed, maybe his hole leads to the kitchen?
Come on! Follow me!
Smurf! It's as dark as smurf in here!
Hello? It's like we're in an armoire!
Nobody to the left...
Nobody to the right...
!?
Okay! Let's go!
15

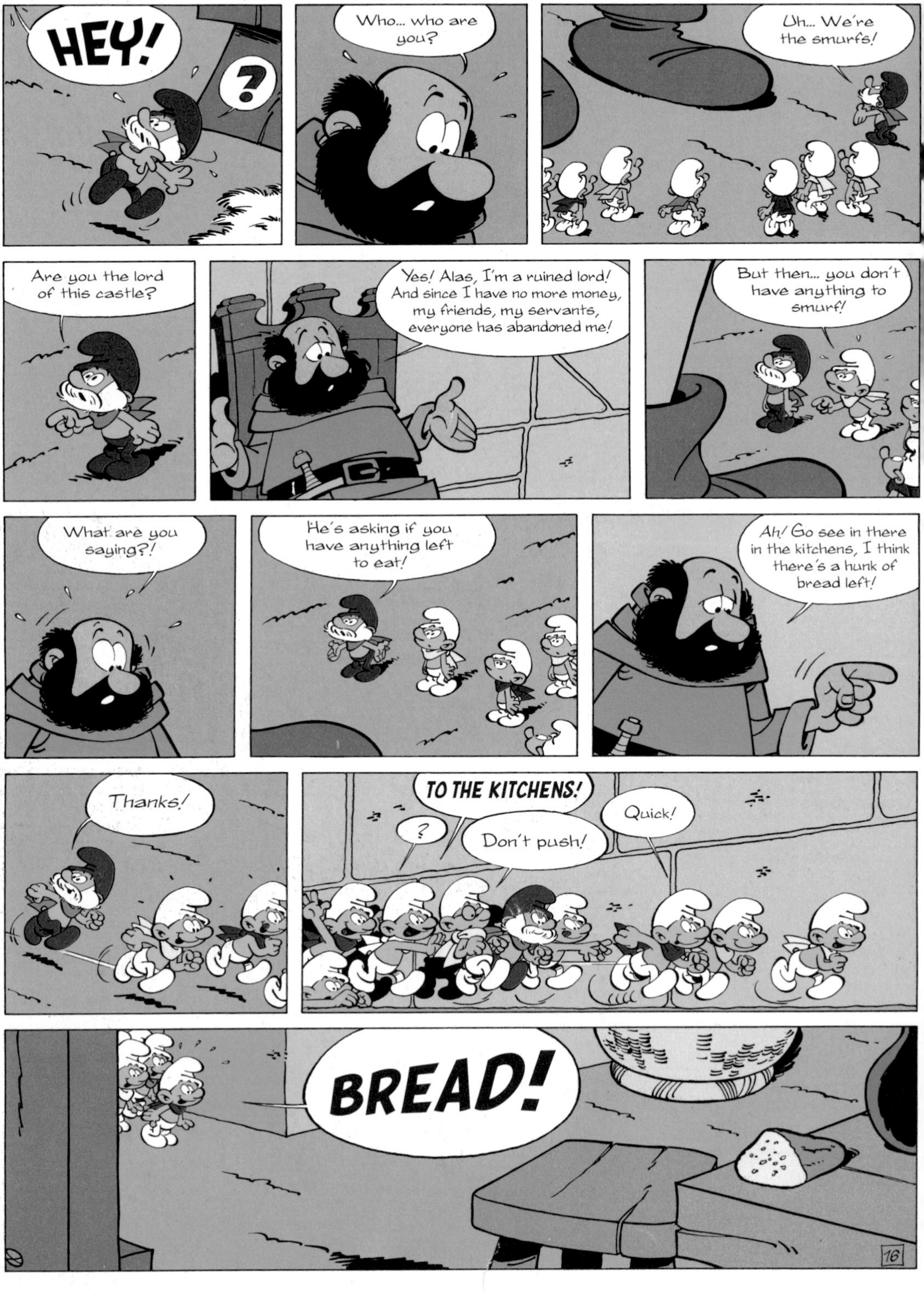
HEY!
?
Who... who are you?
Uh... We're the smurfs!
Are you the lord of this castle?
Yes! Alas, I'm a ruined lord! And since I have no more money, my friends, my servants, everyone has abandoned me!
But then... you don't have anything to smurf!
What are you saying?!
He's asking if you have anything left to eat!
Ah! Go see in there in the kitchens, I think there's a hunk of bread left!
Thanks!
TO THE KITCHENS!
?
Don't push!
Quick!
BREAD!
16

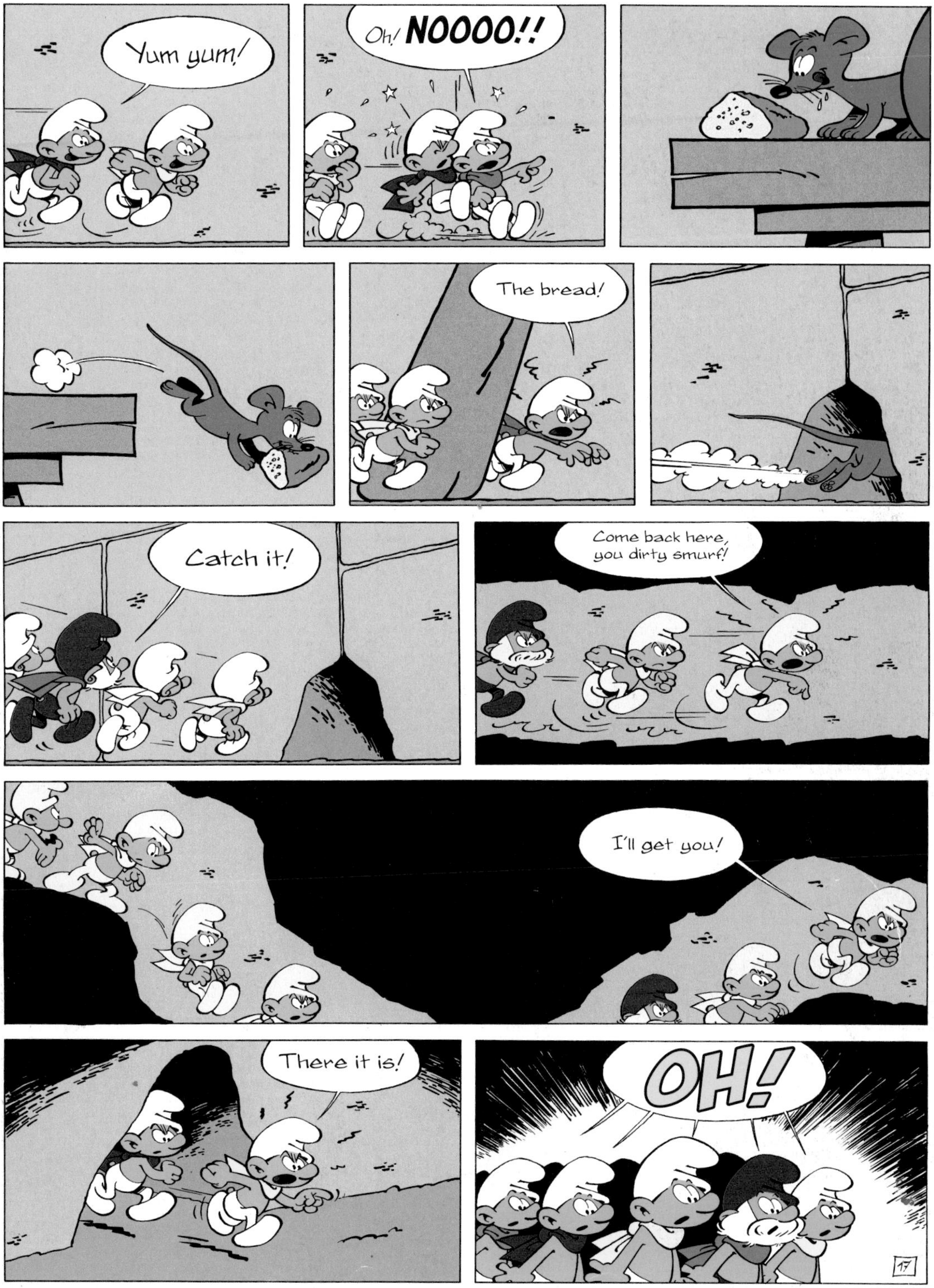
Yum yum!
Oh! NOOOO!!
The bread!
Catch it!
Come back here, you dirty smurf!
I'll get you!
There it is!
OH!
17

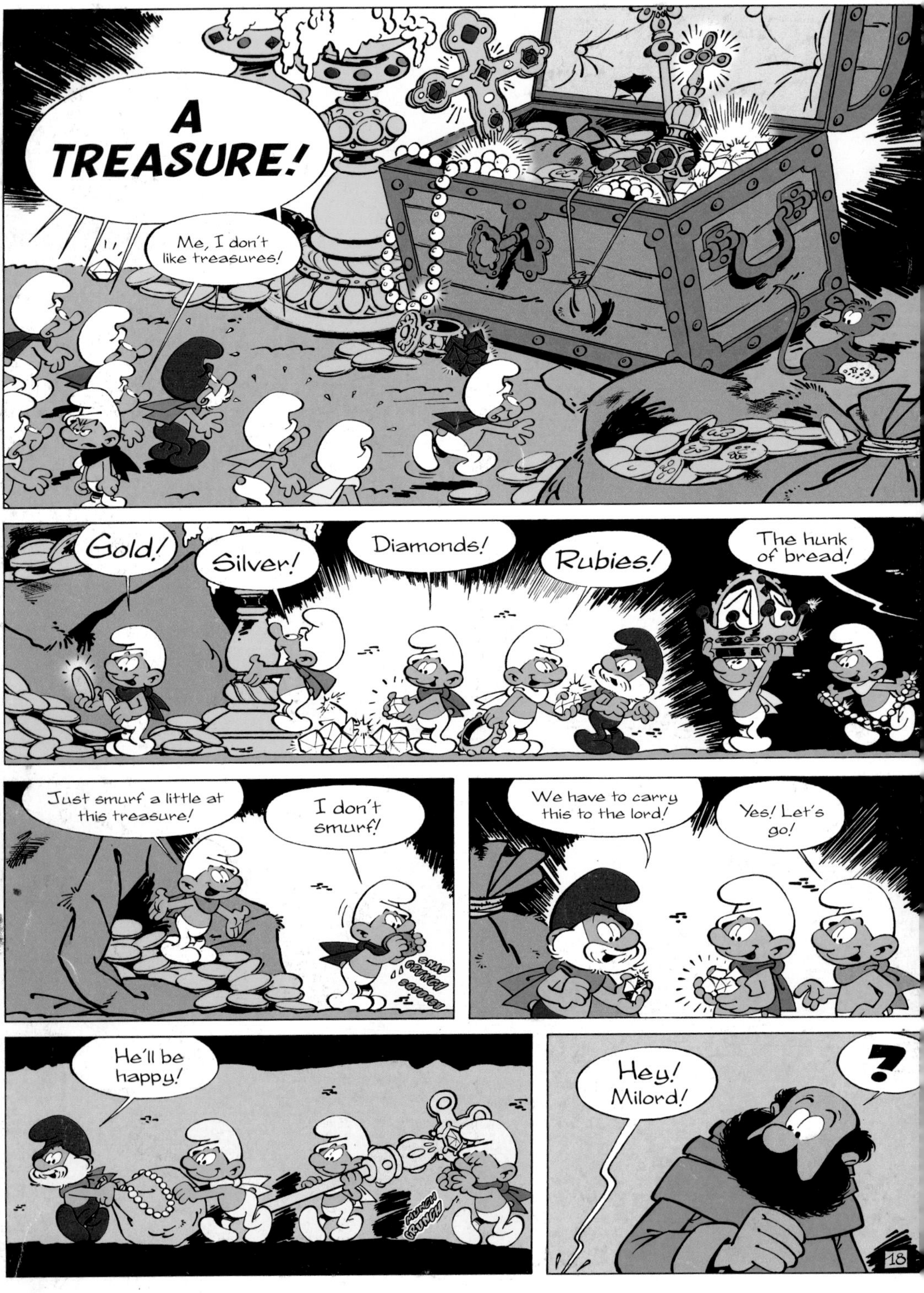

A TREASURE!
Me, I don't like treasures!
Gold!
Silver!
Diamonds!
Rubies!
The hunk of bread!
Just smurf a little at this treasure!
I don't smurf!
SNAP
CRUNCH
SQUOOSH
We have to carry this to the lord!
Yes! Let's go!
He'll be happy!
MUNCH
CRUNCH
Hey! Milord!
?
18

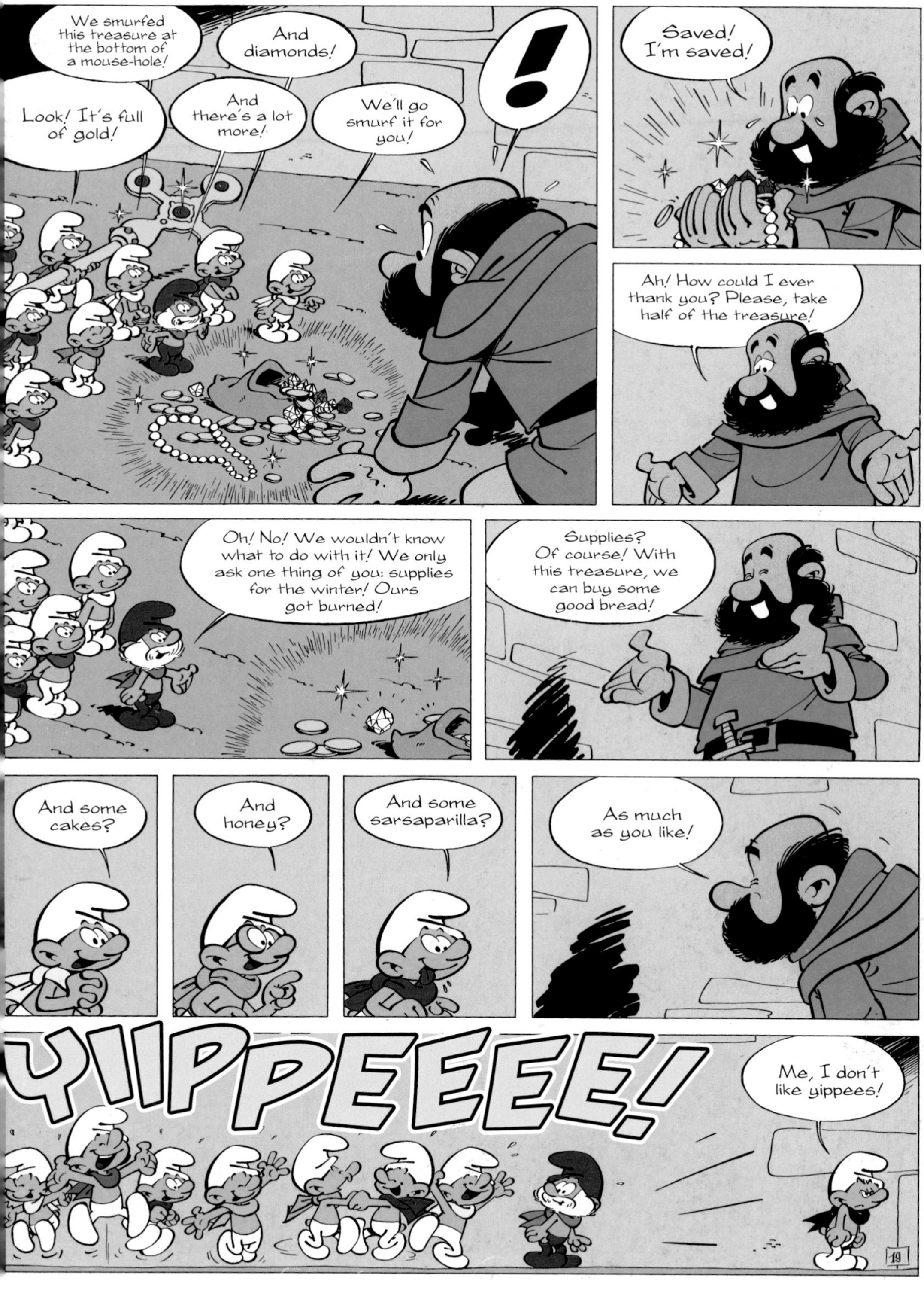

We smurfed this treasure at the bottom of a mouse-hole!
Look! It's full of gold!
And diamonds!
And there's a lot more!
We'll go smurf it for you!
!
Saved! I'm saved!
Ah! How could I ever thank you? Please, take half of the treasure!
Oh! No! We wouldn't know what to do with it! We only ask one thing of you: supplies for the winter! Ours got burned!
Supplies? Of course! With this treasure, we can buy some good bread!
And some cakes?
And honey?
And some sarsaparilla?
As much as you like!
YIIPPEEEE!
Me, I don't like yippees!
19

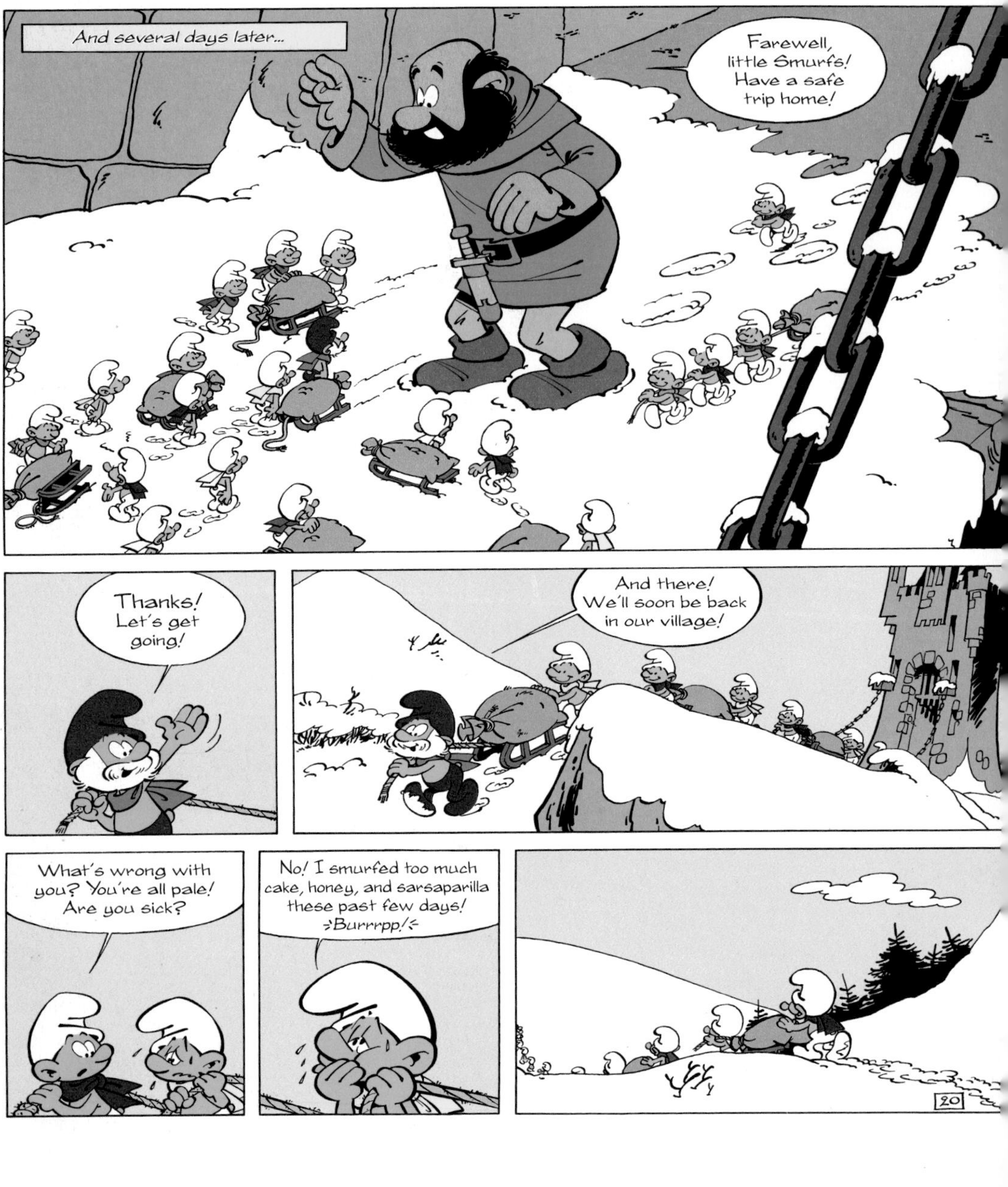
And several days later...
Farewell, little Smurfs! Have a safe trip home!
Thanks! Let's get going!
And there! We'll soon be back in our village!
What's wrong with you? You're all pale! Are you sick?
No! I smurfed too much cake, honey, and sarsaparilla these past few days! ≠Burrrpp!≠
20

And that was the **END** of the Hungry Smurfs.

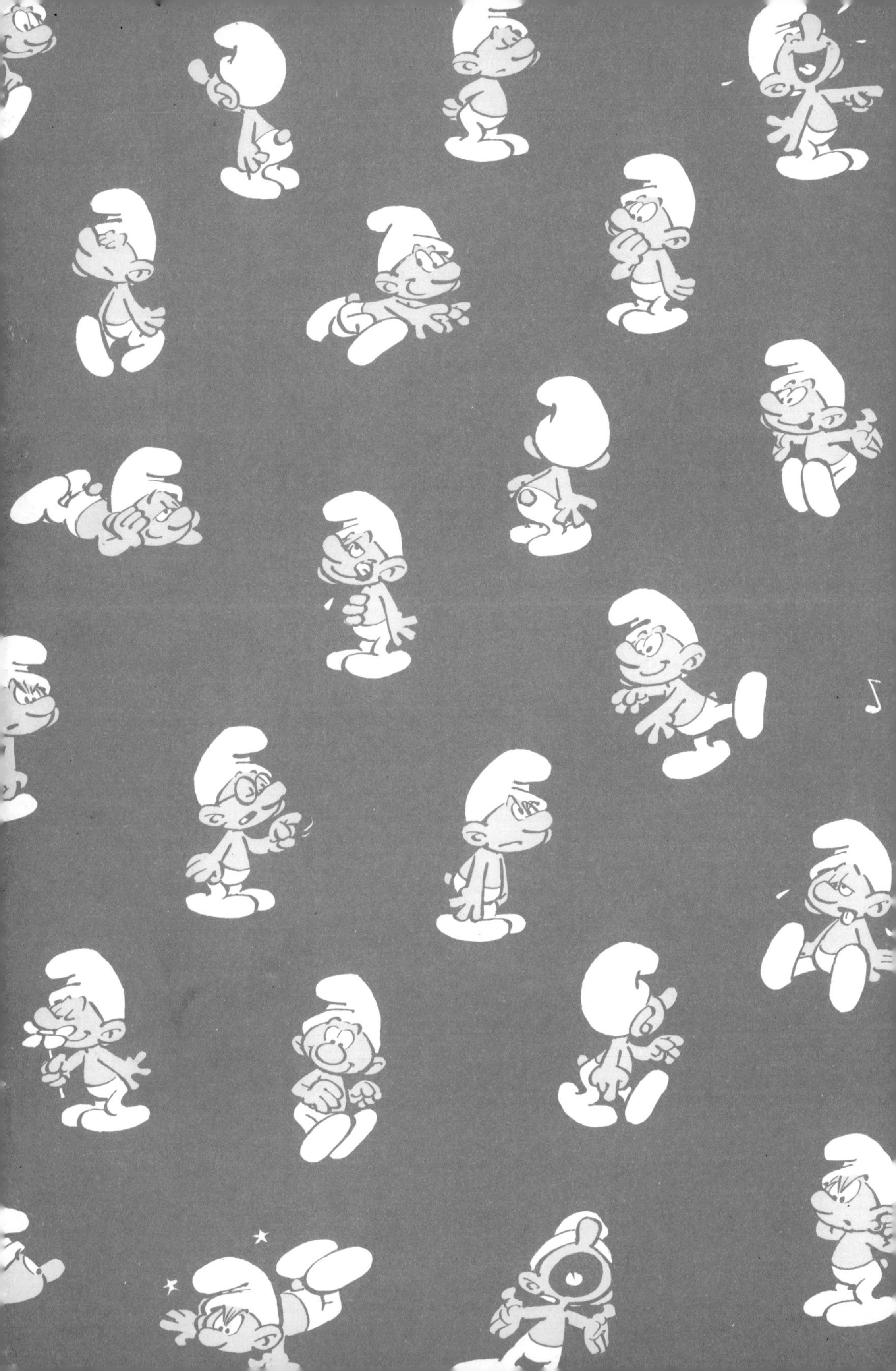